THE RIVER IN SPRING

LESLIE PIKE

Copyright 2021 Leslie Pike

All Rights Reserved

Without limiting the rights under copyright reserved above, no part of this publication, may be reproduced, stored in or introduced into a retrieval system, or transmitted, in any form, or by any means (electronic, mechanical, photocopying, recording, or otherwise) without the prior written permission of both the copyright owner and the above publisher of this book.

This is a work of fiction. Names, characters, places, brands, media and incidents are either the product of the author's imagination or are used fictitiously. The author acknowledges the trademarked status and trademark owners of various products, brands, bands, and/or restaurants referenced in this work of fiction, which have been used without permission. The publication/use of these trademarks is not authorized, associated with, or sponsored by the trademark owners.

Editor: Virginia Tesi Casey
Proofreading: Michele Ficht
Cover: Kari March, Kari March Designs

For Cynthia,
I feel you in my soul. You are a spectacular woman.

1
Nobel

Can you be called a Peeping Tom if you're on your own property? Either way I have no intention of looking away. Arrest seems a small price to pay. Besides, the stranger has to take some of the blame. Yesterday, even from a distance, I could see the woman's part in my undoing as a lifelong introvert. What made her guilty couldn't have been more obvious.

It was the honey colored skin-tone, forcing me to come up with descriptions like honey colored. The blonde hair, escaping from under the wide-brimmed hat as she fished. One long wavy strand, and how it made this man's imagination swell. I become bold in my dreams. In bed last night I thought about the sun-kissed curl. How I would wrap it around my finger and give it a tuck under the brim. Yes, I'd like to tuck her.

That is why I'm heading back to the high spot at the edge of the spread, binoculars around my neck. That detail alone would prove premeditation. At times being an attorney is a buzzkill. Feigning ignorance is no defense. There is no hiding from the fact behaving like a stalker is wrong. As easy as it was to reach that ironclad conclusion, I am just as sure to ignore the inconvenient truth. In this case I will do what I want. Nobody will ever know.

For the first few yards, Maudie has been my shadow. I am surprised she's made it that far from the house before taking a seat on the grass. Maybe there is a fear if I don't see her, she'll be forgotten. Never. The late morning air is still crisp, and it makes the pain worse. My hound is like an old woman with sagging jowls and sad eyes. Never far from the ache of arthritic joints.

The limp is getting more pronounced, but she pushes to keep up. I take it slow. A best friend deserves that mercy and anything else I can do to make her last months bearable. Fucking cancer. Dogs should be exempt from an illness so ravaging, just by virtue of the fact they love without conditions. Their loyalty seems purer than ours. Why didn't a God reward that?

I give her a rub and a few kisses on the snout, then move alone across the field of newly blossomed wildflowers. The scent of that purple flower growing everywhere is heavy. Forget its name, but I have seen it bloom in springtime for twelve seasons now. It appears for just a short time. All the most beautiful ones are like that.

This is my spot. If man feels the call of one setting, this is mine. I have hidden from life here before when it was required. And now, I cannot picture living anywhere else. The only thing missing is a woman who can love a loner. A nearly middle-aged man set in his ways looking for *the one*. But the flaw in the plan is there is no plan. She would have to appear out of the mist or come knocking. And being able to live like this only works if you are of the same mind. *Good luck with that*.

Reaching the thicket of trees, I weave my way through. She accompanies my thoughts. Again. It keeps happening. As soon as my eyes opened this morning, images of the mountain girl came. It's odd a stranger can occupy so much space in an already crowded mind. I haven't even had a good look at her face yet. Maybe the fact we will never know each other has captured my attention and made this two day obsession explainable. There is no harm in looking. Appreciating.

Yesterday I spotted her camped on the river running through my land. Normally it might have pissed me off. But the laws of Montana, as they pertain to private property, are on the fisherman's side. With the purchase of the property the realtor made sure it was known. If they can access a fishing hole by way of a public road, it's theirs to use. That's only half the story. There is only one way down from the road, and it is not an easy trek.

Got to give it to the girl. In the years I've owned this place, only one other person put in the hard work it takes to reach the fishing spot. That was seven, eight years ago at least. The white-bearded baldheaded man looked like he could fight a grizzly. The image fit the task.

The fact this woman carried supplies for at least a two day trip is impressive by virtue of her size alone. By the time I spotted her, a tent was pitched, a fire pit made, and a place to clean the fish organized. She's got mad skills.

I come to the scene, and angle myself between two trees for a good view. Luckily, the sound of size thirteen footsteps doesn't carry down the incline to the river's bank. The rushing waters muffle any crunch of stones that might reach there anyway.

I am just high enough above and far enough away from where she stands in the shallows. A psycho killer would find this place perfect for hiding. Shit. Comparing my habits to a murderer isn't a good sign. At the very least, if she turned and spotted me, I'd look a fool. But that unlikely scenario isn't going to stop me. After all, my mother didn't give me the nickname The Invisible Man for nothing.

I was a quiet, sneaky kid, who liked observing things without anyone knowing they were being watched. It was a superpower over my brothers who didn't realize I was gathering evidence in case they tried to rat on me for something to take the heat off themselves. That happened regularly until my sneakiness caught up with their blame game.

So I raise the binoculars for a better look. With a confidence that must be born of experience, she casts her fly. Think that's what they call it. My zero experience with fly-fishing makes this interesting. Out of my box. It's not just her looks that appeal, it's how well she's navigating the river and the command of the rod. I'd like her to command my rod.

There's no hesitation in her movements. It's pure confidence. By the look of her body, I'd say she's closer to twenty than thirty. But that could be because she's so physically fit. Great ass, honey. Legs too. Thankfully, she doesn't have waders or a boxy shirt on. Cut-off jean shorts, a sleeveless white t-shirt under a fishing vest, and sturdy boots ankle deep in the cold water complete the picture. Bet her nipples are hard. Nipples.

This sexy, sporty, just happens to be younger than me woman, can handle the wild outdoors. That's fucking hot. And, what does age matter? She could be a hundred and twelve, and I'd still be looking. The fact I am forty-three doesn't factor in the story. *Damn hat*. Take it off and turn around. Let me see your face.

The rod bends. Hard. She's hooked one! I've never been so happy for a fisherman. Fisherwoman? Who cares? There's a trout on the line. There's no show of excitement. Only calmness, like it was expected. I'm more excited about the catch than she appears to be. In a flash of movements, the fish is reeled in squirming. What a beauty. She lifts it to the sun and appreciates the catch. The sky is a perfect blue. This would be a great photo for the good life in Montana.

Wading back to the shore, where the camp is, turns out to be a show. The muscles in her calves and thighs are awesome. Man. She squats on the riverbank. Doesn't seem like it's any effort to sit in that position. Fantasies of an uninhibited cowgirl riding atop me appear unannounced but welcome.

She unhooks the hapless fish and goes to toss it into a large bucket of water. But then a pause. Walking back to the shore, she returns the fish to the water. Interesting.

Then a prayer I wasn't aware I was making is answered. The hat gets tossed to the blanket laying beside the tent, and golden hair comes tumbling down. Good God Goldilocks. I'd like to have a fistful of that as we fuck each other on the mountain. What is she doing? Damn. The binoculars are hardly helping. She climbs to the entry of the tent situated higher on the incline. All I can see are legs now. She turns. Fuck! I've lost the view just when things were getting interesting.

Then she's gone, ducking into the tent, for who knows why or for how long. If only I could see inside. But at this angle it wouldn't be anything more than legs anyway. Higher. I need to get higher, over the branches that block the show. How?

My sweater comes off and gets tossed on the stones bordering the trees. Pushing up the sleeves of my shirt, I study the way forward. What's the next move? My best bet is to climb the tree leaning over the incline. It looks sturdy enough to support a hundred and seventy-three pounds. Maybe seventy-six after the ice cream I've had this week. And last week. Maybe the week before too. Now that I think about it, it's a staple. My hand wraps around the nearest branch and gives it a shake to test the sturdiness.

Then the most unbelievable thing happens. Mountain Girl comes out from the tent, and although I can't see above her thighs, I think she may be in a swimsuit. I always was able to see the edge of the shorts before.

Oh hell yeah! She starts stretching. *She's fucking stretching!* And what my will is up against is revealed, like a golden nugget among a pan of grey pebbles. Her legs widen and she bends to touch her toes. Right side, left side. Just kill me now, because there's never going to be a better sight than this. Naked as the day she was born. Neked.

She takes a step forward. I get a better look. Teases of her face, firm small boobs, and a full bush pussy like the bunnies in my grandfather's old Playboys. My first masturbation prompts were full bushed women. Just sayin'. She could bring it back.

Then the universe decides to double-down on its gift. The remarkable becomes otherworldly. Squats. One. Two. Three. Four. If I remain conscious it will go down in my life as the most unexpectedly exciting moment. The binoculars get readjusted. That's it. God Almighty, thank you for this remarkable gift. I will *never* lose appreciation for this moment. What did I do to deserve this? Obviously, I suffered a horrible death in a previous life and now I'm being rewarded with a glimpse of pussy heaven.

I'm frozen in place, maybe in the throes of an illusion. A fantasy. A lust filled dream. All three. One thing is real. My dick is getting harder by the moment. Fact. Never again will I see such an innocently erotic scene. Even if I live to be a hundred. I'd love to applaud and whistle my appreciation, but that would blow my cover.

So I climb, like an ape in the jungles of Africa who just picked up the scent of the female in a tree. Hand to limb, legs wrapped around branches, I rise. It's not quite as easy as it was back in the day, but I'm getting the job done. This one's a little out of my reach but I think I can grab on if I can stretch far enough. Shit! Ripped the shirt. So what? Keep going. I aim for a strong branch that angles to the right. There's a good view from there.

But when I swing my leg over and take a seat, it's blocked by the foliage of another branch. It's not quite as thick as the one I'm sitting on now, but it looks strong enough. Think so. Shit! She's walking into deeper water. Seventy-five percent of her rocking body is on display, and nothing of the face. Need to get on the other limb. Very carefully, I move from one to the other, making sure to keep quiet as I do. This is an undercover job worthy of the sneakiest fictional detective. Sometimes you have to bend the rules to uncover the truth. It is a job for The Invisible Man.

I make it across, one rough limb to another, just as she enters the river. Now I see it all. Wow. For a mountain girl she's very feminine in her movements. She relaxes into deeper water. Perfectly muscled arms and graceful fingers take easy strokes. As she turns over to float I see all of her. Great face. All American natural beauty. She's young and sexy and I'm a pervert sitting in a tree.

There's an expression of contentment on her face that can't be faked. Even from here it's obvious. If I can just edge out a little further, I would have an unobstructed view. No matter how far she swims. Inch by inch, leaf by leaf, it takes a full minute to get in place. Ah. That's perfect. I'm a genius.

The sharp cracking sound of the branch, about to give way, is the unmistakable clue. I freeze, hoping stillness will save the day. It doesn't. The branch and I fall in one unit, as if I'm part of the tree.

The fifteen foot drop is cushioned by the incline. But on the way down my body connects with every lower branch and outgrowth. And for some stupid reason it feels like everything is happening in slow motion. Face, ribs, shoulder, ass. No body part is left untouched, and I feel the jabs and stab of the sharp edges.

Slamming into the earth is harder than I remember from my football days in high school. It comes at me in real time now, and the sound of man versus hill gives me away. Slowed by the impact and soft mud, I slowly slide headfirst to the shore. Peripherally, I see movement in the water.

"What the hell?" she yells over the river's voice.

It's not fear I hear, but anger. Don't blame her. Shit, am I in one piece?

"Sorry. I'm really so sorry," I call from face-plant position.

I'm too embarrassed to raise my head and look at the girl. Close ups of stones in mud are a better choice. Maybe if I just lay here contemplating the pebble poking against my nose it will all be a dream. I try becoming invisible. It's not working.

"If you know what's good for you, you'll stay down till I'm out of the water. I've got a rifle and I'm not afraid to use it on a guy who gets his jollies hiding in a tree looking at naked women."

It's a command. The sound of water splashing as she moves quickly to the shore gives me a few seconds to form a story. Let's see. What can I say? The binoculars lay a few feet away. There's just one shot at selling the lie. I come up on my elbows but stare straight ahead.

"I'm a bird-watcher. Thought I could get a better look at the Yellow-Tailed Warbler I caught sight of. It was a rare sighting this far North."

That sounds feasible, right? I point to the binoculars, but as soon as the words leave my mouth I'm acutely aware of how pathetic they sound. Like I made up a bird name. Which I did. God, I'm screwed.

She calls from the tent. "For a bad liar and a deviant, you don't look like a pervert."

"All men are perverts," I admit.

Footsteps on the shore.

Her unexpected laughter fills the space and echoes off the

canyon. I turn my head to see Mountain Girl with a hand covering her mouth. Jean shorts and a boxy checkered shirt cover all the good parts. She closes the top button.

"Yellow-Tailed Warbler. Good try."

When we lock eyes it's impossible to ignore the humor in the situation. Laughter rises in me. It's pretty funny. And I'm one lucky guy. She's taking the whole thing really well. There's not one mention of arrest.

"Come on. Admit it. There was no bird. You were sneaking a peek and you fell out of the tree. I'll go easy on you if you just tell the truth."

There's a smile on that sweet face, not an accusatory frown. Interesting. *Your honor, I'd like to enter into evidence the plaintiff's expression.*

"Okay," I say, relaxing for the first time. "I was taking a walk, and I saw you. Can you really blame a man?"

There's no reason to tell her it's my property. Instead, I give my best forgive me smile. She's not charmed.

"Yes I can. And I do." The expression and tone have suddenly turned serious. The laughter has stopped.

"Oh. I'm really sorry. I mean, I'll get out of your way."

I regroup and attempt to stand, but my fucking ankle is shooting lightning bolts.

"Not so fast, Mr. Peepers. I'm going to need your name."

The reality of the situation settles. Oh shit. I'm screwed. I'd run if it was a possibility. Just hightail it along the river and double back to my place. But she's got me. *Fuck!*

I stop trying to get up on my own and make the case for forgiveness.

"Wait. Let's not go there. I know you have every right, but if you'd just bring me that chair over there, I'll get up and leave you to your fishing. Please. I'm really sorry. It was stupid of me."

I sit up straight and run a hand through my hair. A twig

with one leaf falls to my shoulder. She's watching and deciding the next move.

"What's your name?" She says it with a frown.

"It doesn't matter."

"Yes it does."

Now what?

"You put me in a vulnerable situation. Now I'm going to do it to you. Tell me your real name. I have all the time in the world and the ability to follow you wherever you hobble off to."

The choices flip through my brain. There is only one.

"Nobel. My name is Nobel."

"You're far from noble."

She's got me there.

"It is. But spelled differently. What's yours?"

"Dove."

"Dove? Like the lovebirds? Very nice."

I get a side-eye for my transparent effort to sooth the beast who has me in her trap.

"I stand by my opinion. It's a good name," I say.

"What's your last name, Nobel? And if I were you, I'd be very careful with my answer."

"Are you threatening me, Dove?" I half-smile begging for mercy.

"Yes. I believe I am. And no court in the land would fault me for doing it. Remember who here is the man hiding in the tree and who is the vulnerable woman legally fishing."

Unfortunately for me, she's right. I know it as an attorney and as a logical human. So I decide to do as asked. Lay it all out and beg for mercy.

"I'm Nobel Lyon, and that's the truth."

Her eyes scan my face and if I'm not mistaken they take in the rest of me too. Dirty and disheveled as it is. It's surprising my statement is accepted without pushback. She even brings the folded chair to my side and steadies it with her hands and feet.

"Try to get up."

With a tilt of my head and an eye to eye connection, I question her satisfaction with my answer. She understands the meaning.

"I did my due diligence when I decided to fish here. I looked up whose property I was going to access."

"Impressive."

I'm not just impressed with her digging, but with the use of due diligence. It's unusual.

As I attempt to stand, my next question rises without thinking it out.

"May I ask how old you are, Dove?"

"How old are you? I'd like to know if the reason you have to climb a tree to look at a woman is because you're going through a mid-life crisis."

I could start laughing right here, if it wasn't for the stinging insult just lobbed over the net. Maybe it's the grey temples. She thinks I'm old. Way to wound a man. I touch my heart and fake a fatal stab.

She giggles. That doesn't suck at all. It almost makes up for what was said.

"I'm forty-three. Now if you think that's old, it's your lack of experience with men. You're young, so that could be the case."

"Touché. But I never said anything about you being old. I don't think any woman would look at you and say that."

"Okay. You redeemed yourself. Now answer my question."

I make it upright and try not to reveal just how messed up my ankle feels. This excruciating pain doesn't affect me. Macho posing bullshit.

"I'm twenty-nine. Not so young or lacking in experience as to make me a freak."

Maudie's weak bark sounds from the top of the incline. When we look, she is scoping the way to make it downhill to be certain I'm okay.

"No, girl! Stay there! Shit! She followed me!"

I try to take a step, but it's impossible without help. The dog places a paw on the incline and tests the first step down. Dove reads my expression of concern. I'm going to need help.

"She's ill. I don't want her to try to come down."

"Stay here. I'll get her. And do what? Is your place close?"

"Thank you. Yes, through the thicket of trees and across the field. You can see it clearly. You'd be willing to do that? After I did, well, you know."

Her stunning smile answers. The brown eyes do too, like sunlight through a bottle of whiskey. Despite my recent collision with earth, I feel gravity losing its hold.

2
Dove

It's not just the old hound who watches. The younger one does too. Climbing the incline, I feel his stare landing on my ass like a laser beam. *Zap.* Don't mind it. Not a bit. As he found out, I'm a free spirit. A woman who swims naked for her own pleasure. In fact, here's a little wiggle. Right now he's wondering if I did that on purpose.

Watch all you want, Nobel Lyon. I've already decided to trust you.

It isn't because I checked you out online before planning the trip. Or because you are my version of physical perfection. Tall, dark, sexy, and a little shy. Well, maybe that's ten percent of the reason. But ninety percent is how you love your dog. Grandpa would say you could tell everything you need to know about a person by how they treat their animals. And when Nobel told a little of Maudie's story, it touched my heart. There was love between the words.

Reaching the top of the hill, I lift myself upright. Maudie slowly pads her way over. The cold nose against my bare leg sniffs a hesitant question. *Can you be trusted?* Her tired head angles to get a look at the stranger, and cloudy eyes scan my face for signs of goodness.

"Hello, Maudie. I'm Dove. You're a pretty girl. Yes, you are."

My outstretched palm gets a sniff and a lick, sealing a hesitant approval. As we turn to walk off, she stops and gives one final look at her human.

"I'll meet you there! Just go home, girl," he calls from the river.

He's talking to the dog. Oh, my heart just melted a little. With a wave, he starts for the hidden pathway known only to him. Looks like the walking stick is working fine. That was one of my better ideas. We unloaded the ammunition and wrapped the rifle in the blanket. Luckily, Duct tape is always included in my gear. I easily find the sweater left behind, then head through the trees. In a few minutes a sliver of an open field comes into view, and then the whole picture.

"Look at all the beautiful flowers! Do you like smelling them?"

Maudie is used to human to dog conversation, because she does the same thing Poko did whenever Grandma asked him a question. He'd stop and make eye contact. Just in case the words walk or treat were about to be part of the conversation. He wanted to be ready. The spaniel's big brown eyes would plead the case. Grandma could be played like a violin by her furry friends.

"You're going to get something special when we get to the house. Promise, girl."

The violin plays for me too.

As we come out onto the field of wildflowers, I'm taken by the riot of color. Each blossom known to me and appreciated. I could give a course in the botany of Montana. Or at least write an article on the flora of the state. Every day, in prayer, I thank my favorite people in the world for teaching me to see and appreciate the beauty we live among. It is everywhere you look. Flowers, trees, herbs. Having the knowledge has been a wonderful addition to my life. Even if all I do is bask in their glory.

"There it is," I say to the dog.

Nobel asked that I take it slow for Maudie. But it's the hound that picks up the pace. Her eyes are locked on the beautiful log house up ahead.

"Wow. Not what I expected."

The home sits on a clearing that borders the open field. It's dramatic and kind of majestic looking in an American way. The first thing you notice are the expansive windows, which offer wide views of a glorious scene. The Yellowstone River and Paradise Valley are on display in a three hundred sixty degree view. The Absaroka Mountain Range acts as backdrop. Gorgeous.

This home, a two-story copper roofed dwelling, is the most beautiful house I've ever seen. That's an understatement at its finest. Who wouldn't want to live here? The wide two step entry onto a wraparound porch greets in the most welcoming way. Substantial wooden chairs, with thick cushions, sit waiting for an audience. Like orchestra seats in a theater, they're front and center facing the vistas. Though each cushion is a different hue, they relate in variations of earth tones, moss green, golden amber, the russet of autumn leaves.

Maudie has her own path to the house. A ramp rises from the ground to the porch, and the hound knows the way. She heads for a large sheepskin dog bed to the left of the front door, and curls in a comfortable position. Like a Queen assuming her throne, she surveys her kingdom. Taking the steps onto the porch, I walk to the end and round the corner. I'm curious to see what the front view is.

I inhale at the sight. "Oh!"

A rush sweeps through me. Like a ghost. No. More like an enchanted spirit. There is something special about this moment. This spot. I'm looking at something my soul finds familiar. These are the kind of feelings I pay attention to. Grandma had the gift, and I do too. I've always thought it could be explained easily. It's a common gift, but only some pay attention to these instant perceptions. Most don't.

For a while all my senses are enhanced. The scent of the blossoms, sun on skin, the call of the regal hawk flying overhead. Appreciation is easy. It bubbles up and comes out in a smile.

When I turn around, the two-story window gives me a peek inside. Cupping my hands I try to get a better view. The glass is treated, and it's hard to see details, but what I can see is the oversized furniture pieces, and a huge fireplace that rises high. I'm going inside.

Retracing my steps, I open the unlocked door. Maudie follows me inside. Wow. First impressions count and this one is one hundred percent positive. The first thing my eyes settle on is the stone fireplace that reaches the second story. I think a person could almost stand up inside. Stunning.

The entire room is an open space, the living room, kitchen, dining room, all can be seen on entering. A wide desk and a high-end office chair sit angled with a view to the outside. Three monitors and a closed laptop take up part of the surface. It's very neat. No paperwork. No drawers. Where does he keep the paperwork? He's an attorney, as I found out in my digging. An organized one I see.

The dog has made it across the living room, to the stone island in the kitchen. She stands frozen, staring at the legs of the perfectly angled barstools in front of her. For a moment I'm stumped. *Is she having a problem?* But then I see the lidded glass container of dog biscuits on the counter. Smart girl. Nobel's sweater gets placed on the back of the maroon leather chair, as I pass to the kitchen. Once the lid is removed, Maudie lifts her head and takes a step back, nails clicking on the wood floor.

"Here you go, sweetie."

The biscuit is gently taken and carried to one of her "spots". It looks awfully comfortable there on the rug in front of one of the leather chairs. I'm guessing it's where the human sits every night. I can picture the idyllic scene. A snifter of brandy comes to mind. No. That's not who he is. Maybe a whiskey.

My attention lands on the far dining room wall across the kitchen. It's covered in photographs. But this is no half-baked display put up randomly. It's well thought out. Each picture framed in the same way, and professionally. How did he space them so perfectly? Black matte wood against the light grey wall stands out.

Oh, this is going to be fun. It will give me a good peek into Mr. Lyon's world. I lean over to catch a look out the side window. Is he coming? Not yet. Good. Let the snooping begin. There's not a lot of time. My first impression is he's from a happy family. The older couple have a kind of cool chic style. The man wears Uggs and bracelets. My kind of people. There's a picture of Nobel and his siblings from the eighties. Three brothers and two sisters. So cute. The two teenagers in the next picture must belong to one of them. Lookers all. There is one sister grown, with another man and one of the kids. All three wear big funny hats.

Dogs. These people love their animals. That's a good sign. This could take me an hour to look at all the pictures and glimpse his life. Why am I not seeing any women? Odd. Only one of the brothers stands next to a woman. And that's an old New Year's picture from two thousand and twelve.

I could get sidetracked here. Think I'll save the photos for last. I need to take a look around first. No one will ever know. Anyway, I'm pretty sure he couldn't accuse me of crossing any lines of privacy. After all, he was spying on me first.

So I head down the hall, looking at a guest bathroom, and two bedrooms that share another full bath. Nice. Where does he sleep? Neither of these say master bedroom, or even show one thing out of place. Okay, guest rooms. Is there time to go upstairs? If I got caught it would be embarrassing. Not quite as embarrassing as falling out of a tree, but close.

Do it!

I exit the hallway and take the stairs two at a time until I reach the landing. When I look back, Maudie is watching. Good thing she can't talk. There's a wide open space with a bar, a big flatscreen, a game table, and six chairs. Looks like a poker table if I'm not mistaken. So he's a card guy. Cool. I can play a mean game of Texas Hold 'Em.

Quit wasting time!

I head down the hall to the one room it leads to. Are those horns I hear heralding my arrival? Double doors are closed, but that doesn't stop me. I swing them both open.

"Ohhh! Jackpot!!"

I expected a pristine bedroom. Not a pillow out of place. Instead, I'm greeted by an unmade bed and discarded clothes at its foot. There's a half-eaten bowl of popcorn sitting on the side table, alongside a beer bottle. Obviously he was in a hurry to spy on me this morning. I have to chuckle. But there's no time to waste.

First I run a hand over the pillowcase he didn't sleep on. Yep. The man knows and buys quality. That's one in the plus column. Actually the plus column began at the river. By now, I'm on number one hundred. A giant flatscreen on the wall opposite the bed is another. This man likes his TV. Most women I know don't like one in the bedroom at all. That's where I part ways with my gender.

Moving to the bathroom I'm surprised by its size and general awesomeness of the space. Never have I seen a bigger shower. Or a better one. It's big enough for four people. Fancy water heads point in every direction, and black and grey tile stacks high.

"Cool."

Dare I open his medicine cabinet? *Hell yes.* It's set into the wall, modern in design and large. What's he got in here, a years' worth of cologne? Opening it, my eyes scan the tidy shelves for surprises. Tylenol, floss, deodorant, all the usual players. Two prescription bottles. Xanax. *And what's this one?* Viagra! These are both old prescriptions. It was filled two years ago. Both look like they are almost full. Well he is in his forties. Didn't know that would happen so young. What's this huge bottle? Gas pills!! What the hell? Why does he need an industrial sized bottle of anti-gas pills? I can't stop laughing.

A sudden urge to pee grabs my attention. At least I'm in the right room. I find the nook, push down my shorts and sit on the fancy toilet. Obviously it's a bidet, but what are all these other choices? This is like the James Bond car. Maybe there's an ejector button, or a secret weapon hidden. He could get rid of a lingering guest or defend himself against intruders.

Maudie's bark lifts to the second floor.

"Oh shit!" I yell.

I finish my business and reach for my shorts. They're up and zipped in a few beats, before running out of the room. At the bottom of the steps, the dog sits looking out the window. The sound of heavy footsteps on the porch stairs announce his arrival. Her tail is swinging back and forth at what she sees approaching. *Shit times ten!*

I hit the floor, and slide into the leather wing chair just as the door swings open.

"I made it!" Nobel says, stepping inside.

"Are you in pain?" I say, noting the pinched expression and an out of breath voice.

I rise and go to him, taking the rifle. Maudie gets a head scratch and a conversation from her guy.

"Hey, girl. Have you been entertaining our guest?"

"Sit down. Rest your ankle."

When he looks up at me I kind of melt with the effect. He is one sexy looking hunk of man. His heavy dark eyebrows knit together but the corners of his mouth lift.

"Your cheeks are flushed. And you're out of breath. Have you two been wrestling with King Kong?"

He gestures toward the soft monkey laying curled on the floor. It takes a few beats before I can come up with a reason that he might buy.

"No. We actually just got inside, because I thought I'd look at the view from the porch while Maudie was taking a rest on her doggie bed outside."

I swear the dog is calling me a liar. Those soulful eyes ratting me out. Then she proves it by walking to the edge of the island counter and looking directly at me. Payment for her silence, canine blackmail at its finest.

"She wants a cookie. That's where I keep them," he says, innocent of my crime of entering and snooping.

"Oh! Let me get her one."

Maudie gets her treat, the second in twenty minutes, and takes it to the spot in front of the chair.

"Come sit with us," Nobel says, hobbling behind the dog and taking a seat in the chair I imagined him occupying.

I push the matching ottoman the last few inches and stand by as he lifts his leg and sets it down. A sigh follows.

"Let me help you with your shoe," I offer. "You should take it off. Here."

He lets me untie the knot and remove the boot. This man has some big feet. Hope that theory holds.

"Let me get the other one. You don't want one shoe on and one off."

There's a restrained smile on his face.

"What?" I say, smiling myself.

"I'm not sure. Except to say this all seems funny. I never expected you to forgive my..."

His voice trails off and his eyes lower. The embarrassment is very sexy.

"Thank you," he offers.

The shoe gets dropped to the floor and I make eye contact. "We should have a look at your ankle. It may have to be wrapped."

"Do you know anything about twisted ankles? It wouldn't surprise me. It seems you're good at lots of things."

My fingers wrap around his foot and the sock gets removed.

"I probably know more than you do. My grandparents were big believers in self-reliance. I can't count the times we handled scrapes and cuts and minor mishaps ourselves."

"Is that who raised you?"

"Yes."

I examine the foot and its ability to rotate. Only his clenched teeth give him away.

"That hurt? Right?"

"Just a little. Think I just need to rest it tonight. It'll be fine tomorrow. Thank you, Dove."

"Yeah. I don't think you're completely out of commission. Just temporarily hobbled. Nice feet, by the way."

The surprised expression on his face turns to embarrassment. But it doesn't stop the man from getting sassy.

"Well thank you. I hadn't planned on showing you my naked foot for at least another month."

I rarely feel shy. But this is how it feels. Shy and happy at the same time.

"Listen," he says, sitting up straighter. "It would be great if you would join me for lunch, out on the patio. I'd like to at least thank you with a meal before you get back to wrestling a bear or whatever you have planned for the rest of the day."

It takes one point two seconds to consider the offer. My wide smile answers.

"I'd enjoy that. But let me help you up."

"Hand me that walking stick by the fireplace. The parents brought it back for me from one of their trips."

I retrieve the tall carved stick and help him upright.

"Do you like lasagna? I made some last night."

This guy is a constant surprise. What else is he good at?

A half hour later, we are under the Montana sky, enjoying a feast. A big romaine salad made with tomatoes from his garden pairs perfectly with the pasta. He added avocado, dried cranberries, and candied walnuts to top it off. Who is this guy that uses candied walnuts? The men I'm used to have been more the order out types. Musicians have their art on the mind almost all the time. You're lucky to get a plate and a paper towel napkin.

Leaning back in his chair he looks at me and smiles. "I bet you're the kind of girl who sees dragons in the clouds."

"I am that girl."

"Tell me Dove, what are some of the things you like?"

I could think of a hundred right off the top of my head. But let's make this interesting.

"I'll tell you mine if you tell me yours."

"Done."

"Old books."

"New books." He smiles.

"Breakfast for dinner."

"Yeah, me too."

"Sunrise."

"Sunset. But both can be beautiful with the right person."

"Songs that *get* me."

He thinks for a moment. "People that *get* me. This is fun."

"Clean fresh sheets."

"God, yes."

"Here's a good one," I say, leaning in. "Change."

He doesn't skip a beat. "Stability. The familiar."

We pause to soak in the revealing information about the other. I look around us at the colorful landscape.

"Flowers of all kind."

He pauses for effect. "Sycamore trees."

"Sycamore trees," I say in agreement.

"Let's have a toast," he proposes, raising a glass of lemonade.

"What shall we drink to?"

"How about weak tree branches?" A gorgeous smile accompanies the words. Talk about feeling weak. That would be my knees.

The clinking of crystal seals our agreement. Sometimes the oddest detail in a day is the signpost on a new path.

3
Nobel

"I would have given my left nut to see that!" Aargon says between forkfuls of chocolate cake with chocolate frosting.

"Falling out of the tree wasn't part of the plan, but I don't regret it."

My father gives me a thumbs up. A big blue-sky afternoon has the birds singing, in our parents' backyard patio. A hummingbird dive bombs my head then flies off to the feeder. It's a good place for the family to enjoy my brother's forty-sixth birthday. The menagerie of dogs running around the giant Oak reminds me of past celebrations and other dogs loved.

Somehow we lucked out with pets. The Lyons won the even-tempered dog lotto. Even though when they are together, the dog cousins' energies change. Like kids do whenever they gather. It's a squad. They become their wild thing.

If it was just Scarlett's dog, that would be another story. Boo and Maudie are buds, and both have quieter dispositions. The Beagle/Whippet plays well with the Hound. But in this instance, leaving my dog at home was the right decision. Quiet time is more important than attending a dog rave.

We sit around the long wooden table, where we have gathered a thousand times before. Feeding our faces and making each other laugh are favorite pastimes of the Lyons. But for the last two years memories of our collective heartache always take their place beside us. Fresh wounds still bleed on a regular basis. Maybe someday far into the future it will be easier to bear Kristen's death. I hope so.

For now, we try to be strong for each other. That's the secret of surviving tragedy, I think. We have had to pretend for Sam's sake most of all. Part of the pretense involves some sense of normalcy.

We didn't drop the ball this year. Aargon's cake is a masterpiece. The Lyon kids' tradition started when Aargon and I decided to make a cake for Van's tenth birthday. That first one was epic. The best part was my mother was all for it. She actually thanked us for helping. Until she saw it that is.

Unveiling it at his party was an important part of the joke. The little shit was always pissing us off and getting away with it, so we decided to send him a message. We baked a lopsided cake and wrote across it, *Happy Birthday! You Are Ten and Have A Small Penis.* He went crazy and cried. But in a twist, he proved us wrong a few years later during a pissing contest. His old friends still bring it up every so often.

Besides getting punished for our creative outlet, it started a lifelong game where we try to up the last birthday cake. All the siblings confer and then decide on the perfect message. It has kind of morphed to include things my parents said to us as kids. The funny stuff. Kristen was the best at coming up with old memories. But together we dig deep.

Today's offering sits half-eaten, but the message is indelibly etched in our minds. When Van carried it out everyone busted up. It was something we heard my mother say one million times as we'd drive to school. And it was Aargon specific. At least at the beginning it was. He may have started it, but Van and I, Kristen and Scarlett picked up the ball and ran it into the ground. I can still see the frustration in my mother's eyes in the rearview mirror. *Whoever is singing the theme from Jaws is going to get slapped!*

Remnants of lunch and unwrapped presents crowd the table. Alongside Aargon's plate, blue tissue paper, held down by a glass of champagne, bleeds onto a napkin. Being able to revisit your childhood home is something us kids love. Referring to yourself and your middle-aged siblings as kids is stretching believability. I have a feeling we will be "the kids" forever. None of us want our parents to ever move from here, and we've told them as much. We have even vowed revolt should they get the urge to sell and travel the world. Van promised to tie them to the Oak like he used to do for fun when he was six. Think he was only half-kidding.

Aargon looks pleased with himself. It's pretty rare to see him so chipper. His dry sense of humor is one of his best traits. I've never known an adult so glad to be having a birthday. Our mother did an excellent job of making us believe it was a special occasion for the world. I'm thinking it will be the same when he's ninety. If he ever remarries, she better get onboard the birthday train.

My falling out of a tree while spying on a woman has everyone surprised. That I told it shocks me more than them. It's the story of the day, which gets me the title and a corner piece. The fact it does not sound like me makes the telling more interesting, especially to my siblings. And they don't even know the good part. Naked details were conveniently left out.

"You're lucky she didn't call the cops. What were you thinking?" my sister says, pointing to her head and laughing.

"Pretty sure he was thinking with the other head, Scarlett," Van says with an eye to Teddy and Sam, his sixteen-year-old teenage nephews.

They both laugh at their favorite uncle. Think a little Coke snorted out Teddy's nose. I remember how that burning sensation felt. The comment does not upset the women. Not an iota. When you are a household of three brothers and a father who says whatever comes to mind, nothing shocks.

My father pushes his plate away and signals for more coffee as my mother circles the table pouring.

"Magnifique! You did the right thing, son. A woman is attracted to a real man!" He lifts a tightened fist. "One who is bold. Am I right, Aurora?"

My parents are odd. They actually like each other and have stayed in love for decades. It's a high bar to reach. Aargon had it with Katie. Forget Van. He'd rather fuck every available woman who agrees to the suggestion. He will be a bachelor forever. Maybe into the next life. Only Scarlett has achieved the goal with Parish, and their relationship is relatively new. I haven't even tried. The shallow end of the pool has been fine. Lust, infatuation, friendship, but never love. Not as I saw it in our home. Not as it still resides there. What's the rush?

"Gaston, I couldn't have said it better. Be bold, children. Look what it did for your father and I." She ends with a kiss to dad's head as the coffee is poured. He answers with a spank to her ass.

"Oh!" She chuckles. He probably has spanked that ass a million times over the course of their relationship. But she still acts surprised, and he likes the reaction.

It starts a whole conversation about how they met in France, when my mother was traveling through as a young woman. Boldness factored greatly into their beginning. On both sides. We all have heard the stories of my grandparents' pushback when they learned their brilliant daughter, with a chemical engineering degree, had fallen for a poor French artist without a pot to piss in. *My God, Aurora!* I can hear my grandmother's plea to the heavens as she retold the story.

Then when they saw the new boyfriend, how their fears multiplied. His hair was halfway down his back and wild. According to my mother he was sexier than a bohemian Oliver Reed. I had to be shown a picture to know who the hell that was. Then I got it. The grandparents were no match for that kind of smoldering energy. Us kids could repeat every story of their meeting word for word. But it doesn't mean we don't enjoy hearing it again.

"So tell us about the lucky girl at the river," my biased mother says. "Was she touching her hair when you were talking?"

Sam and Teddy look confused. I explain.

"Body language. It's like a "tell" in poker," I say. "No. I didn't notice her doing that."

"What does she look like?" Van asks.

"Blonde long hair, brown eyes. She's about 5' 3", but her confidence is 6'4."

"Nice. Does she have a sister?"

Van is always on the lookout for new contestants in his game of Anything But Love. He chooses women like himself. Neither party interested in the long-term. He currently is in between women, but that won't last. Not just because the ladies like whatever he's got, but because he can't go without female companionship for long. His dick would fall off.

"I don't think she has siblings. Her grandparents raised her. I don't know the entire story yet."

The table takes a pause in conversation.

"Yet?" my mother says.

There's trouble keeping my interest hidden. No one here is fooled by my attempt at coolness, least of all me. I've kept details of any relationship I've ever had mostly to myself. Why did I just think "relationship"?

"We're going out tomorrow night," I say, hoping it's the end of conversation on the subject.

That starts a whole thing. I just sit back and watch as each person digests the news. My membership in The Loner Club is in danger of being revoked. Rarely, if ever, do I talk about a woman I'm dating. It's been like pulling teeth for a family that thrives on conversation. To the person, they love sticking their noses in each other's business.

"You asked her out after falling from a tree spying?" Aargon says. "And she said yes?"

"She wants some of that." Van chuckles.

"That's about as bold as a man can get!" My father looks proud. "It's in our DNA, boys," he says, aiming his comment to his grandchildren.

"We came back to the house and had lunch out on the deck."

I knew that one was going to hit the mark, but I couldn't help myself. Dropping bombs can be fun. Stunned faces look at me like I've become an alien. My mother's hand on my shoulder says more than words.

"Don't get excited, Mom."

A wave of her hand dismisses my comeback and quells further comment.

"You took her to the house?" Van says. There's a hint of doubt in his voice, as if such an unbelievable fact has to be challenged.

"Are we being punked?" Scarlett asks.

"Where are you going to take her? Fletcher's Steak House? Mangione's?"

I let everyone get it out of their systems before I answer.

"She's a singer/songwriter in a band. There's a performance tonight, so we'll grab something afterwards."

This new information gets them excited. Again. Shit. Here come the questions.

"How awesome! Where are they playing?"

"What's her name? How about the band? What are they called?"

"Her name is Dove, and I swear to God, if any of you figure out where and show up, it will piss me off."

I'm interrupted by my sister's squeal. "Oh my God, Nobel! We know her! She's the lead singer with Montana! How many people have that name?"

Scarlett punches her fiancé in the arm for emphasis. "Can you believe this?" she asks him.

"I'm as surprised as the rest of you. But good for you, Nobel," Parish says.

I'm the one surprised.

"How do you know her?"

"Your sister may be exaggerating a little. We don't actually know her."

"We had a conversation after one of her shows last month," Scarlett says. "She is so talented. You'll see. Ha! This is really cool! You make a great looking couple!"

Van gets the bad boy look on his face. "Have her sing to you."

When all eyes look to him, he adds, "What? I went out with a girl that could sing."

My chair scrapes the ground as I rise. "It's been great, but I'm headed out."

"No! Stay a little longer. We will stop the questioning," Dad says.

That's impossible for the Lyons. Not my father nor anyone here are able to deliver on that one.

"Thanks for the meal, Mom. Happy birthday, brother. Are you old yet?"

It's the question I've asked Aargon every birthday. Being

two years younger meant more back in the day. I figured my big brother would tell me when he was grown up. Then I'd only have two years to wait. Now it's turned poignant as we get closer to leaving youth behind permanently. It's stretching the truth to say it hasn't already happened.

"Almost. Maybe by next year," he answers, not skipping a beat.

My relationship with my siblings has always been either, 'I'll help you hide the body', or 'don't even breath in my direction'.

Their protests and promises fade behind me as I leave their company. Did I say too much? Yeah, I did.

I should have called, but I didn't want to give her the opportunity to cancel. Now, as I approach McCandy's, it's real. The billboard shows her smiling broadly as four band members surround her. Montana. That's a good name for a band. All younger than me by at least fifteen years. The guy with his hand on her shoulder is good looking. I hate him already.

People are waiting to get inside. There doesn't seem to be a certain type. I see young bucks and seniors. Couples and singles. A few cowboy hats. Maybe they're a country band. The cold is not a deterrent. Passing the entry, I take my place at the end of the line. Shit. I thought I'd just walk in. Hope I left myself enough time.

Vapor rises from the mouths of people talking. A spring cold front has descended. Girls wrap their arms through the arms of their companions, and more than one person is rubbing hands together for warmth. The two girls in front of me turn.

"Have you seen them before?" the redhead with a green knit cap asks.

"No. This will be a first." I smile.

"See! I told you," her young companion says.

My confused expression prompts the redhead to explain.

"We were playing this game we do every week. We try to put a story to the people in line. You know, just to pass the time. We saw you coming."

"What's mine?"

"First clue is you're alone. My friend here thinks it's because you're a talent scout, or an agent, and you want to see what all the buzz is about."

"What was your guess?" I ask the friend.

A crooked grin preceeds the answer. "I think you just like to look at the singer. Right?"

The line moves up.

Just as I'm about to answer, the burly bouncer I passed at the entry walks up.

"Are you Mr. Lyon?"

It surprises. "Yes?"

"Can I see your identification?"

"What's this about?"

"There's a table waiting."

The girls in front of me are listening to the conversation. The redhead elbows her friend and presses her lips together trying to squash a comment.

"Yeah. Okay. Here." I take out my license and show it to the Hulk.

"Follow me," he says, heading for the entry.

It would not be wise to make eye contact with any of the people in line. It would piss me off too if it were me being cut ahead. Just one female voice is protesting. The bouncer and I ignore the angry words. He says something in the ear of the woman at the front desk, and she motions over the din for me to follow.

I expected a bigger venue. The crowd outside tricked me into thinking it could hold them. This room can be described as modest. The sign at the entry declares a maximum occupancy of one hundred and fifty. The lighting is bright and the furniture dim. But those details don't tell the whole story. Every seat is taken and the servers are busy as drinks are ordered and delivered.

Past patrons have pinned short reviews on the wall to the right of the wooden bar. Pieces of napkins or backs of business cards. There's a square of toilet paper folded neatly with just an exclamation point. I'm too far away to read them, but there's lots of exclamation points. Someone has sketched a sexy girl at a mic, and two words in big, bold, black letters say, *Marry Me!*

On a relatively roomy stage for the space, sits a set of drums, a keyboard, and three microphone stands. Only two have mics in them. The speakers stand guard on either side, cords winding from them like entangled snakes.

I take a curving course through the patrons, following the woman. She stops at the only vacant table in the entire room, and gestures for me to sit. I chose the chair with the best view of the stage.

"A server will be here to take your drink order."

"Thanks."

The retreating figure is replaced by an older woman who comes to my table. I get a broad smile and a hand on my shoulder.

"What are you drinkin', darlin'?" she says over the voices of the crowd.

"Give me a whiskey. Gentleman Jack's."

"You got it. Want me to bring another when I see you need it? It gets pretty crazy in here."

"Thanks. Yeah."

And then the lights dim and the room explodes in applause and whistles. Shit! I just made it. An exceptionally deep voice from offstage interrupts the excitement.

"Ladies and gentlemen, put your hands together for your favorite band, the pride of McCandy's, the reason you came out in the cold ... MONTANA!"

Four guys come onstage to applause and whistles of the crowd. They're young. Everyone looks that way to me at this point. Two carry guitars and walk out playing the intro to their first song. It's a Stones song. We are being teased. That guy I noticed on the billboard is better looking in person. And close in age to Dove. Great news. I smirk.

Whoever dressed him took into account the guns. A tight, white shirt shines a spotlight on them for the ladies. Bracelets are stacked on each wrist. He winks at the blonde sitting closest to the stage and bites his lip. The girl is practically wiping the drool from her face. The guy she's with touches her arm and says something in her ear. Uh oh. Is there going to be an argument?

The other guitarist is dressed to blend with every other band member across the last seventy years. Jeans, a faded T-shirt, the obligatory scarf wrapped loosely around his neck, as if he just threw it on last minute. Kind eyes and a shy smile greet the room.

The drummer is a hard-looking guy, who I picture having a mugshot. He takes his place and doesn't look at the audience at all. Drums sound the beat, and he becomes lost in the music. A tall long-haired guy, wearing jeans and a green velvet shirt, stands at the keyboard scoping the faces in the audience. He points to a couple of people a few tables from the front and gives them a nod followed by a grin.

*Da da. Da da da da da da da da...*there it is. Oh yeah!

Final notes of the intro sound as Dove walks out onstage, singing the opening lyrics of "Jumpin' Jack Flash". When she sings she was born in a hurricane, it lights the audience. The level of excitement rises in every one of us. Hell yes, woman.

Wow! In a beat I'm a crazy fanboy. There's a sexy rasp to her voice. A sultry ache.

The look, and the way she moves across the stage, connects with the audience. Fuck. What is she wearing? It's a great choice. The long golden gown is body hugging. The tight sleeves, the top half of the dress poured over her, then flowing and see through from the thighs down. It follows her every move like a trailing mist. The loose wavy hair and the gown match, and a thin ring of gold stars sits atop her head. Looks beautiful. Like an angel. A Sexy. Fucking. Angel.

Is she looking in my direction? No. That was wishful thinking. Scanning the room, it comes together. The men are mostly in the same frame of mind as I am. They all think she's looking at them. We are held captive to Dove's appeal like worker bees to the Queen. All happy just to be around her.

There's a table of four guys who are moving with the music. If I'm not mistaken, and I'm not because one guy just made eye contact with his tablemate and blew him a kiss, they are gay. Their excitement plays out differently than us drooling heterosexuals. It's the men in the band they're lusting over and the woman whose beauty they appreciate and love.

The women around the room are moving to the beat. When *they* do it, it looks cool. Arms in the air, dancing in their chair, always feeling the tempo. It is organic for them. But for us guys, things can be very different. I was not in line when they passed out rhythm. I look like a big dork dancing. But if ever there was a time to be inspired, this is it. So, I tap my foot and rock in my seat. Just so I don't look like there's a stick up my ass.

When the song ends, Dove speaks to the audience with an ease that can't be learned. She's a natural and comfortable in her art. The band plays a background accompaniment.

"We are so happy to play for you tonight! We're Montana!"

The applause grows as she walks to the bass guitarist. Mr. I Know I'm Hot.

"Give it up for Tony Taylor!"

The women respond as expected, which prompts Tony to play a riff and bite his lip again. She blows him a kiss. Dove lifts an arm in the other guitarist's direction.

"You know Oscar Rodriguez! Send him your love!"

Another great reaction, but this guy doesn't feed on praise. His head lowers with his smile.

"And what about Jimmy Dinkins on the keyboard?"

He makes eye contact with the people in front and sends a salute in response to their whistles and cheers.

"And I know you love our drummer, Z.Z. Casper!"

The ten second drum solo and the response from the crowd makes her point.

"And I'm Dove Solomon," she says, touching her heart with a bow.

Now the sound grows to an eardrum blasting level.

"Let's get moving, shall we?"

The time passes quicker than anyone in the crowd wants. This band cannot be pigeonholed. They played rock and country. They did oldies and some original songs. The keyboardist and bassist sing too and the voices blend well. There was a funny bit introducing her grandparents' love song. The lighting on stage dimmed, and Dove got serious. She layered the sweet moment by sharing she was raised by them, and what their relationship's successful union was built on. She says they shared a love song that inspired them for over fifty years.

Then the long whine of a guitar sounds, and familiar

chords let everyone know what's coming. An anthem for every generation since the sixties. Dove calls out, "Wild Thing!" It's a rallying call that prompts everyone to start singing along. I'm grinning like a crazy man. This is very cool, and it gives me a peek inside her upbringing and the things that shaped her.

About an hour in, she spots me. The acknowledgment she sends with her eyes and soft smile land in my heart. And then, as she takes a seat center stage, the words of Faith Hill's "Breathe" are directed my way. It's not that I'm so sure of myself, or that I'm reading too much into things. It's the strange feeling that swept through me when our eyes locked. Like a gentle wind.

4
Dove

The initial high of performing is usually followed by an energy crash. Splat! Then by Oreos crumbled over cookies and cream ice cream in bed, watching recorded episodes of Jimmy Fallon. Or my current reality program obsession. Tonight, I am officially breaking with tradition. This is a proper dinner. With a man. An actual date.

"Want to hear which song I liked best?" Nobel says, cutting his steak.

"Was it 'Wild Thing'?"

That's the usual favorite of the men in general. No mystery why.

"No. Although that was great too. It was 'Breathe'."

He stops there, not explaining his choice further. Not acknowledging I was looking right at him as I sang. His knife and fork are still in his hands but resting on either side of his plate. He's held the stare and is waiting for my reaction. The ball squarely in my court. Two can play.

"Why that one?" I say, forcing him to put words to feeling.

"Because, well, I kind of thought for the first time in my life I was being sung to."

His head dips as the words come out. As if it took courage to admit it happened. What a doll. He's damn cute for being such a handsome man. So I rescue him from drowning in unnecessary embarrassment.

"You were. Glad you noticed."

Now the head lifts and a gorgeous smile breaks out. "I did. And I liked it."

If anyone is watching us, they are wondering what was just said because I'm certain I look about twelve and he looks sixteen. The boy I like just said he likes me. It feels like happy mixed with embarrassment, desire with excitement. It's a huge ball of emotions. Both of us chuckle, and now I know he feels it too. It takes a few seconds before he speaks.

"So no boyfriend? And please say no."

Chuckling, I answer truthfully. "I've been too busy for a romantic connection. There have been boyfriends, but nothing has stuck. I'm a picky woman disguised as a free spirit."

"A great combination for the *right* man."

That quiet confidence he has? Gold.

"What about you? I'm certain the ladies love you."

"It's not like that. I'm not like that." He says it with such certainty it's hard to doubt.

"What are you like? Tell me."

"I'm a man who finds satisfaction in quietness, solitude. I like my house and my job. I love my family and my dog. I am not a complicated man, in fact, what you see is what you get."

"Have you made room for the one?"

His brows come together as if I've just proposed some novel idea.

"I'd make room if it happened. So far that hasn't been the case. But I was in a long-term relationship a few years ago."

"What happened?"

"She was too much like me. She liked her own world as much as I liked mine. We never made room for each other. Ends up, that isn't the best way to be. Obviously love had nothing to do with it."

"Wow. You are really fucked up."

I hold a straight face for a good five seconds while he questions if he just heard right. Then he sees the devil in my eye. A wide smile lifts the corners of his mouth.

"For our first date this is remarkable," he says. "I'm absolutely sure it's going down as the best one ever."

I lift my glass of Rombacher Cabernet Sauvignon in a toast. He responds in kind. Apparently, this is good wine. It would take a better palate than mine to discern the difference. My lightweight status as a drinker is not debatable.

"To weak tree branches." I giggle.

"And to the woman in the river," he adds.

A sip later, I look up at his eyes. Oh God, he hasn't looked away.

"So tell me about how you ended up being raised by your grandparents."

As he goes back to his meal, I fill in some of the blanks.

"My mother was a single mom. I was about a year old when she passed."

Nobel's eyes soften with my words.

"She was diagnosed with breast cancer while she was pregnant. When she died her parents took me in and cared for me until I went out on my own."

He puts down the utensils.

"I'm so sorry, Dove."

"It's okay. I never really knew her, but I so wish I had. My grandparents kept her memory alive."

"What was your mom's name?"

The question hits me square in the heart.

"No one has ever asked me that. It was Rosalie. Her name was Rosalie."

He just scored major points, even though I don't think he was aiming for that.

"Pretty."

"Her parents became responsible for me and they didn't ever make me feel they didn't love the experience."

"The fact their love song was "Wild Thing" tells me a little about them. Did they teach you to fish? Is that where you got your love of the outdoors?"

"Oh yes. They were old hippies from back in the day."

"That's cool. What were they like?"

"My grandmother kind of looked like Janis Joplin. Even when she was eighty, she had hair down to her waist. Before my mother came along, they lived in a commune if you can believe that. But once they had a child, things changed. They decided to have a more stable lifestyle."

"Did they live here in Montana?"

"Yes. They eventually bought the house I live in now. They were wonderful people. Lived simply, spoke gently, and made their own fun. I feel privileged to have been raised in that environment. We made most of our clothes, and we had a big garden of fruit trees and vegetables."

"It sounds idyllic."

"Many times we fished for our dinner. In fact, my grandfather fished on your land. Right at the spot you found me last week."

Eyebrows knit and his head tilts to one side. "Did your grandfather have a big white beard and a bald head?"

"Yes! How did you know?"

"I think I saw him once. He impressed me because he was older at the time and he was obviously still able to make the trip down."

"He was as strong as a bull."

"And now that I think about it, he had the same kind of reaction you had when he fished. Like he almost apologized to the fish. Kind of a Zen thing."

"That's him! Oh! He used to fish there all the time before you owned the land but he had a heart attack and didn't make it there again for years. That story makes me so happy," I say, a tear suddenly welling and running down my face. "To think you saw him."

We braid fingers. He doesn't say 'don't cry' or get embarrassed that his date is weeping in the fancy restaurant. He stays silent in my grief, standing by me.

"Your sympathy is touching," I say. "You seem to get it."

"It's empathy. My sister Kristen died a few years ago."

"Oh, Nobel. I'm so sorry. That must have been crushing for your family. I saw her picture on your wall."

With a sigh, Nobel lets me inside.

"I don't think I can ever get over what happened. People say you get through it, but I think you end up in a new place. Missing her is just part of life now."

"Same here with my grandparents."

"Do you ever talk to them? I mean out loud?"

I chuckle. "All the time. And I see nothing odd about it."

"We find comfort where we can."

He kisses my hand and that one gesture soothes me to my core. Then I get a brainstorm.

"I have a favor to ask of you. But I don't want you to say yes because I'm teary, or because you want to get into my pants."

A contained smile appears on his face. "I won't, and I do. But we can talk about that another time. Ask away."

That gets him a silent brownie point.

"I still have the remains of my grandparents. I've been waiting to find the right place that would mean something. A place in nature because they were so at one with the land.

What are my chances of sprinkling their ashes on the shore of the fishing hole?"

"I have no problem with that. None whatsoever. In fact, I practically owe it to you."

"Thank you, Nobel," I say, squeezing his hand. "Oh, that's really kind of you."

"Don't be so surprised. I'm more than just a man with questionable self-control."

His hand picks up one of my curls and gently winds it around his finger. He plays with it for just a moment before tucking it behind my ear. His fingers sweeping the edge. Who knew the curve of my ear could be so fucking erotic? Never has been before. I felt it down to my wiggling toes.

An image of kissing him pops in my mind. We are naked in his bed. Clear as day. Not sure if that's a vision or just a wish, because his shlong was awesome looking. I'm going with the second one because if it turns out he has a little pickle that would blow confidence in my gift.

I'm at a crossroads here. If it was a vision, I want to throw every reason not to sleep with him out the window. Why wait? It's already ordained. Why shouldn't I be the aggressor? But it's important to remember he may not be there yet. Just because I saw it, doesn't mean he has.

My Devil self is making her case on one shoulder, while my wisest Angel across the way is simply filing her nails listening to the argument. Can't hurt to consider all options. Can it? That fucking white winged know-it-all. Every time she's silent I know I'm going to do the *right* thing. The safe thing. The thing that will protect me in some way. Damn brain.

"Where'd you go?" Nobel asks.

My daydream dissolves instantly. I'm a little embarrassed.

"Sorry. I was just ... You might catch me doing it again." I chuckle. "You don't know yet, but I have this sort of sixth sense. Once in awhile I get a fleeting picture in my mind, or a certain feeling. I know it sounds crazy, but I respect it."

He gathers a question before speaking.

"Did you have a feeling just now or see a picture?"

I'm surprised he takes the news so well. As if it is a given. I learned early on to only share my gift with certain people. It can be misunderstood. God help the man who belittles it. But Nobel has taken it in stride, so I continue.

"A picture. It's nothing bad."

"Tell me."

Oh shit. Now what? My mind flips through my choices.

"I prefer to keep it to myself. Because sometimes I can misinterpret what is seen," I lie.

He doesn't press for more details.

"Okay. I think it's impressive that you're so in touch with your feelings. My mind is usually on a case, or the dog. The hundred things I mean to accomplish in a day. Maybe if I paid more attention to unusual images, I'd know what it feels like. I'm kind of a straightforward man as far as emotions go."

"That's a good quality. *Know thyself.* The ancient Greeks were right."

I'm rewarded for quoting my favorite maxim with a look that says he likes me. He likes me.

"I knew you were pretty, and that you are a hell of a performer. But Dove, I want to tell you I think no matter how long we talk, I'd never be bored."

"That may have been the best compliment I have ever had. Thank you."

"Welcome."

The server comes to our table and breaks into our conversation.

"Can I take away any plates?"

"I think we're through. Dove?"

"Yes. It was delicious," I say to the young man.

"How about dessert? Did you save room?"

I look at Nobel and he nods.

"Definitely. Bring us a menu and I'd like some coffee."

"Me too."

"Absolutely," he says, gathering the dishes.

The server leaves with plates on one arm and our empty wine glasses in his hand.

"Tell me about your career. What kind of law do you practice?" I ask, genuinely interested.

"I'm a Document Review Attorney. Sounds boring, I know. But it has been really rewarding and interesting. To me anyway."

"What exactly is that? I've never heard of the specialty."

"I evaluate documents for other lawyers. I analyze data to determine if it's relevant to their particular case," he says. "I told you. I'm weird."

"It sounds like you like being internal. Finding how things connect."

He liked that. Right before smiling, his nostrils flared just a little. Sexy boy.

"You understand," he says a little surprised. "It's good because I can work from home. I did the whole downtown office thing for ten years, before I bought the property. Then the draw to stay put was too strong."

The dessert menus and coffees are placed on the table.

"I recommend our lava cake. But it does take a good twenty minutes to prepare."

Nobel looks at me. "Shall we be bad?"

I feel my own horns rise. The server waits and watches our dance.

"Let's."

This time I twirl my own hair.

. . .

Answer! Answer. I need her take on the latest news. Come on Deborah, I know you're there.

The click of the connection lifts me.

"Hey gurl," she says. "How was the house tonight?"

"Quit thinking like a manager and start thinking like my best friend. God, I thought you were missing in action. This is the third time I've called this facacta landline."

"I'm coloring my hair. Didn't hear it. What's up? Nobel?"

"It was one date. It's not like that."

"What the heck does that have to do with it? I know you. Do not forget who caught you and my brother with your pants down. Maybe that's when he figured out he was gay!" She laughs hysterically at her own joke.

"There is the small part of the story you're leaving out. We were five."

"Details. He's still a horn dog. You're still the same girl. Me too. We don't really change from our young selves."

"True. He was checking out the guy in the front row tonight."

"Of course he was. They probably already did it. So how was the date? Did you have fun?"

I kind of melt into the memory.

"Oh, it was really, really, really fantastic. He's such a cool guy, Deborah. Smart, and nice. Sexy as hell."

"That's what I wanted to hear. How come you're home so early?"

"It was a long day. Besides, Nobel has a sick dog and she needs medicine at certain intervals. The dog is terminal."

"Ohhh. That's so sad."

"They're best friends. I kinda love that he's that way."

"Did he try to hookup?"

"There were signs he wanted to. But desires were controlled."

"Why? Boom chicka boom," she sings.

"I can't put it in words. Except to say it's like it was too important to rush."

I hear the intake of her breath. "God. Did you see something?"

My friend knows me well.

"Maybe. But I may have been wanting it so much that I created the vision."

"I'm not buying it. You have never misread things before."

She's got a point.

5
Nobel

Our phone conversations are getting good. I have wanted to be the guy who says all the right things. Who wears confidence like a perfectly tailored suit. What man doesn't? But in the past talking romance when you are in two different places hasn't seemed natural. When your default setting is invisible, you can't easily reset. I'm more the guy to prove his worth in person.

Dove is playful and never shies away from my feeble attempts at bringing up the fact we need to fuck. The urge has overtaken us both. We have danced around the elephant in every room. In prior conversations, with other women, I always have had to involve alcohol. My words sounded flat and it took me out of the moment. With her it's different. I put a crumb out and she picks it up and makes a soufflé.

Words are all we have. Date number two waits in the wings. The band's two week trip to Nashville for a booking has made calls mandatory. With each one we stretch the boundaries of decency. She seems to be enjoying it as much as I am, and that is one appealing quality. Being indecent is highly underrated in women. But they are the only ones that misjudge the advantage over us drooling primates. Men are aware.

In the meantime, one restrained kiss will have to hold. Never went so slow in my life. Not at any age. There hasn't been reason enough to wait. Until now. It sucks to know it is part of our story, because the risk of losing the moment is real. Wouldn't want to be a man forgotten before I give her a reason to be remembered.

At first, I attempted controlling the voice of my libido. No matter how loud he was, I was in charge. Calls were once a day and involved news of her recording session of the band's latest original. I asked all the right questions and showed the genuine happiness I feel for them. That business is brutal. She told me that. Yet it's who she is and where she wants to be. I'm going to support her just as I want to be supported in my interests. The difference is mine take place in my house in front of a computer screen and hers involve the public.

I didn't want to look like I feel, completely taken. Nobody likes someone who pushes too hard. Needy is not a good look. But why rein in the part of me that feels so fucking great when we talk? Not to mention a dick aggressively reminding me to think of sex with the golden goddess. Like an annoying kid tugging on my sleeve, I ignore him constantly.

It's more than sex. I like how she laughs and the way the sound pulls you into her joy. There is a lightness about her that can't be ignored. And it's more than her youth. The conclusion I have arrived at, is there has been something missing in my life. Don't exactly know how to describe the indescribable thing she brings.

Sitting between all the lofty thoughts is the realization I *need* to fuck her. Need being the operative word. A literal ache is involved, and the cure is Dove. In a kind of weird sense, I know it would be almost ...no, don't even think that.

Pushing hesitation aside, the word spiritual pops up like a neon sign blinking on and off. Never will I say that aloud. It sounds like a guy trying to sell the idea the physical and spiritual are connected just to get laid. I am not. This is the first I have believed in the concept and I don't know what to do with the information.

If we hadn't already talked twice today, I would be calling again. Instead, I use my waning self-control and get ready for sleep. That is the only way to stop thinking about the girl.

The cell sounds. Dove.

"This is a surprise. A good one," I say, happy as shit.

"Thought I'd call you for a change."

"I was just getting in bed. Perfect timing."

"Me too."

I pause for a beat, before jumping into the deep end.

"Wish we were together. I could tuck you in."

"Tuck me?" she says with a naughty tone, followed by a giggle. "Sure that's what you meant to say?"

Here's the moment.

"Did I say tuck? I meant fuck."

The giggle turns into laughter, and I join in.

"At least you didn't hang up, and report me to the authorities," I say.

Slowly, our laughter quiets.

"Now why on earth would I do that?" Dove says in soft tones. "Don't you know I want to be with you too?"

Immediately my dick reacts with a sharp lift. The sheet moves. I stroke myself.

"Get your ass home, woman. When do you land?"

"Tomorrow at two-thirty."

"Let me pick you up. Can you spend the night?"

"Yes."

Alert the media! No. I need to act like that wasn't the best news of the world. *Be cool!*

"We'll swing by your house and get your things."

"Don't have to. I'll have them with me. I'm going to be naked ninety percent of the time anyway. I won't need much."

The world stops spinning. And somewhere the male angels in my crew shout a hallelujah and fist bump all around.

"Dream a little dream of me," she says as we end the conversation.

As if I would do anything else.

The last eighteen hours have passed like a snail crawling on cold cement. Like a sloth climbing a tree. Like me knowing I'm about to have sex with the most desirable woman I've ever known. Time is moving slow as fuck.

I have never been so ready. Not the first time I had sex, or even as a boy dreaming of things outside his reach. My dick has now become speaker of the house.

"Where are you?" I say, scanning the area outside baggage claim.

Talking to the air has become more common lately. Before I left the house, I said excuse me to King Kong when I accidentally stepped on the toy. Maudie looked at me like I was crazy. I blame it on distraction that won't be denied. If ever a female was distracting, it's Dove.

I spot her as she comes out the wide glass doors, blonde hair gleaming in the sunlight. Those jeans look like she was sewn into them, hugging beautiful curves. Syrup on pancakes close. It's the opposite of the airy loose blouse that hints at treasures just underneath. It's not exactly see through, but close. A deep V allows for a peek inside I bet. If you were at the right angle. Those are nipples I sort of see, areolas too. At least a shadow of them. Implying she is braless. Get your ass in the car so I can confirm my suspicions.

Two of the band members are with her. That Tony guy

puts a bejeweled hand on her back and they exchange cheek kisses. I don't like him. A familiarity hints at a back story. But I have no idea if it's an old lover or just a friend. Fucker. Just in case he has designs on rekindling a romance, I am keeping an eye out. The Invisible Man is watching you, dude.

Now Jimmy seems like a standup guy. He's the one who writes songs with her. As far as I can see he's the quiet one. Like me. His goodbye is more in the friend zone. There are no kisses from him. Just a pat on her shoulder before walking away. The judge inside me bangs the gavel. I'll allow it.

As they walk off, Dove turns and spots the car. A wide smile lifts perfectly shaped lips. She runs to me as I put the car in Park and get out. Arms encircle each other. There are no words, just eyes speaking volumes. You would think we were lovers separated for years. With her face in my hands, I run my thumb over her full bottom lip. I take the long-awaited kiss.

Everything other than the two of us fades. The tired kid screaming for his mother, and the announcement over the loudspeaker. Travelers waiting to be picked up by friends become a misty backdrop. There's only her mouth against mine, and the feeling of a consequential piece of life falling into place.

"I've just been kissed for the first time."

Wood lit. Bonfire.

"Let's get out of here."

A half hour and a thousand feelings later we are well on our way. Highway 15 never seemed so fucking long. Somehow the road has lengthened overnight. Like a giant picked it up and stretched it just to piss me off. The illusion seems real. Just my dick's luck to be stuck behind an old van. It scales the elevation like an overweight mountain climber with bad vision. *Come on, people!*

I make a quick decision to change lanes. Passing the slow

as shit car in front of us reveals a happy family of five. They're actually singing to some upbeat unheard song. Three kids in the backseat seem to know the lyrics. Hand signals accompany the music. Being pissed at their speed proves my faulty reasoning. Lust has invaded the thought process, pushing aside better angels.

"Are we almost there?" She says it like a kid approaching Disneyland.

Enthusiasm is appreciated. It's what I'm feeling too.

"Five minutes more," I say, looking at her face. "Have I mentioned how beautiful you are?"

"No." She grins.

"Well it's true."

"Want a little preview?" An eyebrow raises for emphasis.

My dick weighs in its unanimous consent.

"God yes."

Pink painted fingers roll up the hem of the blouse. Slowly. While she hums the stripper's theme song. Fuck, it's got me mesmerized. Bronzed skin, flat stomach. Oh, a belly chain. That's hot as hell. My hand reaches out and jiggles the delicate golden chain. Just a few more inches until the big reveal.

Right when I'm about to get a glimpse of the twin treasures, the van behind me honks its frustration. Shit! A glance at the speedometer confirms the stats. I'm only going thirty. Now I'm the mountain climber blocking their ascent. I add one descriptive word. The *horny* mountain climber.

Dove starts chuckling, and it's contagious. The blouse returns to its rightful place, covering her breasts.

"Maybe that wasn't such a good idea. Let's just get to your house in one piece."

I make the turn onto the property and from the rearview mirror I see the family continue their happy journey. If little cartoon birds were surrounding the van tweeting an accompaniment I would not be surprised. And something more. For the first time I feel the call of that kind of joy. Maybe it does exist.

No more fucking around. Get to it, man. I start removing my sweater. Holding the steering wheel with my knees, I maneuver one arm free and then the other. Over my head. It gets tossed in the back. At first, I have an audience. Until I move to the buttons on my shirt. Then I am joined in the unveiling. Dove kicks off her shoes then unbuttons and unzips the jeans. What? You'll play? Oh yeah! This woman gets more inside my head with every new thing learned.

When my shirt falls to the seat, she runs fingers over my chest. It's fucking exhilarating. The feel of a delicate hand brushing my nipples is like a feast to the starving man. I reach between her legs. My middle finger traces the seam, up and back. Up and back.

"I can't wait to kiss those lips."

She lifts and pushes down the denim, revealing a delicate white lace triangle that covers what I want to see. She is out of the pants and watching my face as she does it. There's some happy little tune accompanying the reveal. I cannot speak. Excitement has rendered me mute. My heart is about to explode. 911 emergency.

Her seat gets reclined, and one silky leg lifts and a foot settles on the dashboard. She runs a finger over her slit, to tease. Mission accomplished. Then she pulls back the panties. The bush is gone, and in its place the most gorgeous smooth pussy awaits my touch. I have never been with a woman so free. Oh God. Her eyes lower and then lift to mine.

"Want to kiss them now?"

In the history of rhetorical questions, that is number one. I stop the car where it is, alongside the field of grass and riotous wildflowers. I can see the corner of the house, but it might as well be miles away in another county. Shutting the motor off, I unbuckle the seatbelt, and head for heaven. I take in the clean scent of her, before my tongue finds the softness and fingers part the way. A pink, wet, welcoming thing of beauty awaits the lustful attention I have to give. Glistening juices are beginning to show.

"Your sweet pussy."

That's all I can get out before going back in.

"Ohhh. Lick me," she sighs, head resting against the seat.

I do as asked. As demanded by every impulse. My will to please her is great. Want her to want me in equal measure. Taste number one. The pink clit is poking out of the hood. Undeniably the center of the Universe. The tiny marble that sits on the throne demands my attention. Even though we just met a minute ago. I worship her with my mouth, tongue, and lips and absorb the sounds made by her pleasure. A moan that will never be forgotten. An intake of breath. So real and raw.

When our eyes meet she grabs a fistful of my hair. "Show me your cock."

The words spill out of luscious lips. Then, she giggles. It's a command I follow, raising my hips and pulling down my jeans and boxer briefs all in one. A grateful dick escapes the bondage of my pants and lifts in her honor. Luckily, I do not come empty-handed. Fingers encircle me and just the touch alone is so exciting a bead of cum appears as evidence. There's surprise on her face.

"That's what you do to me."

Licking it off, she shows me the proof.

"Nectar of the gods."

"That's it. Get out of the car," I command.

We're laughing at our impatience. I *need* to fuck her. She *needs* to fuck me. Here on a grassy bed, against the hard metal of the car or in the backseat. Before we combust. Or I prematurely ejaculate and she spontaneously orgasms. It could happen.

Exiting the car I trip. My shoes are still on and my pants are halfway down my legs. Why the fuck did I wear these fucking shoes? With laces! Idiot!

Her laughter rises as she comes around to my side and sees my predicament. The girl wears only a blouse. And hoop earrings. I begin to quickly disrobe, and she does too. The first look at her breasts is breathtaking. Pink areolas, prominent nipples ready for sucking, and champagne glass sized orbs. Perfection. I'm like a baby finding the only source of nourishment for the first time. Give it to me.

She rises on painted toes and does an impromptu dance as I get my shoes and pants off. The swing of blonde hair follows her with every turn. The Fucking Fairy of Spring performing a ritual. Turning her back to me, she wiggles a high, round, awesome ass in my direction.

I think of grabbing the blanket in the trunk. Not going to happen. The second I'm out of the last remaining article of clothing, I turn and take her in my arms. The kisses are on another level. A hot, wet, deep place known only to those who have felt burning passion. Standing skin against skin butt naked in the sun, with Montana's big sky above us, feels like what forever means. It just keeps getting better. The smell of her skin. The taste of the kiss. How she moves and looks. She surrounds me.

Her fingers thread in mine.

Looking into her eyes, I say, "Want to get some grass stains on that beautiful ass?"

We move onto the field and find a level spot for nature's bed. It's perfect. Soft and firm at the same time. The scent of flowers and green grass. She is underneath me, arms over her head. My grip around her wrist tightens. Every one of my senses charge. I lean in and kiss her slow. Then, my lips against hers, I say, "Fuck me."

How could I deny this feeling? It is in my heart and in my mind. The strange part is she inspires me to keep thinking about it. In this moment I am the opposite of The Invisible Man. I want her to see it all. This is a connection I've never felt before, and it's making me want more.

6
Dove

The sky has darkened to deep purple and tangerine, and the wind has picked up. Its low long whistle reaches across the field. Time has been stuck on sex o'clock, but my guess is we've been out here for three or four hours. A ladybug just flew off my chest, where she had found a soft landing and a good view of the show. A signal to go inside.

Nobel reaches out a hand and pulls me upright. I feel the effects of having been naked and not afraid in the elements. The afternoon sun left its mark on the bits of me not used to exposure. There is a knot in my hair, the size of a golf ball, at the back of my head. It was made tight by the back and forth rhythm of head against ground while being ravaged. Rats would find it a good nest. Bits of grass are imbedded in my knees and ass. And I'm sure my lipstick is smeared off and whatever makeup I wore long gone.

But he is looking at me as if I'm the most beautiful thing he has ever seen.

"The property is properly christened now," he says, bringing me close for another kiss.

When my eyes show doubt, he continues. "It's true. I've always been able to make it to the house." He chuckles.

"I need water. And a comb," I say, touching my knot.

"I need to piss."

"Why don't you do it? You're not going to be arrested for peeing on your own land."

He doesn't need more encouragement. Making a half turn, he gets to it. I'm watching the penis. This time it has nothing to do with sex.

The professor in me comments. "Very interesting."

A laugh proceeds his words. "Haven't you ever watched a man taking a piss before? Am I your first?"

Now I laugh. "No! You do not hold that honor," I joke. "But it looks like there's two streams coming out. What's up with that?"

Giving it a shake, he shows me the evidence. "Didn't you notice?"

There are two distinct holes at the tip of his cock. When I look closely, it is really one with a connection of skin in the middle, which makes for two streams.

"Magic." I say it using jazz hands.

"Come on, Houdini. Let's go to the house." A shake finishes the job. "You can continue the tour of my penis there."

Continue? Lordy. The man has stamina. He notes my expression.

"Don't you want to?"

I slap his naked ass with my open palm. "I do!! After a shower and some food. We must have burned off ten thousand calories."

"That's my girl."

. . .

As warm water streams overhead, over my hair, and down my back, I think about our arrival at the house. When Nobel came in the front door, my carry on in tow, Maudie's greeting was so sweet. It brought tears to my eyes. The wagging tail and whine of happiness told us her feelings. Her breath was slightly labored as Nobel bent to comfort his friend. I could tell it bothered him.

When he asked me to go ahead and shower first while he gave the dog her medications, it was no surprise. He put Maudie ahead of himself and before our passions. Good man. I could see how much the dog relies on him. Seeing fear in an animal's eyes is heartbreaking. It reminds me of my grandfather's gaze at the end. There is a stare that looks different. Even the strongest man I have ever known was a little afraid of the approaching storm. I guess most of us will be in the last days. Sigh.

Turning off the water and stepping out, my toes grab at the plush bathmat. The thick white towel waiting in the towel warmer envelopes me. I dry my body then wrap it around my hair.

This solid white terry robe I pilfered from Nobel's closet, per his instructions, wraps me and dries the remaining beads of water. It looks like an elf is wearing the giant's clothes.

Hearing Nobel's footsteps gives me a few seconds to prepare. I untie, hold the lapels of the robe and get ready to flash him. I strike an innocent pose. As soon as he enters the bathroom, I whip it open then just as quickly close it, retie and giggle at my own play.

"Hey now! Hands down that's the best view in the house. Fuck the mountains and river."

But he's wrong. What I'm looking at is a visual wonder. He stands in his briefs carrying a tray of food for us. There's a delicate wildflower trying to stand tall in a glass. Nobel's hair has not been combed yet. He's still barefoot. It looks fucking hot. And more than anything the expression he wears is a reflection of my own state of mind. Happy. Simply happy.

It is magic when you feel your own over the top, all consuming pull being returned. I had not felt this before. I felt it coming at me a few times. I felt whispers of it from me now and then. But never have I been a binary star in the heavens.

"I'm going to shower then we can have dinner in bed. In fact, start without me. I know you're hungry."

He moves out of the bathroom, toward the bed.

"I can wait," I call, taking the towel off my head and using it to dry my hair.

He returns empty-handed, drops his briefs and takes my robe off.

"I didn't want to leave without saying goodbye."

We fall into a kiss that sparks a vision of round two. I feel his cock poke my belly.

"Uh oh. I better get in the shower before I take you right here."

He leaves me with a suck of each nipple, a slap on my ass, and a smile on both our faces.

Ten minutes later, we are eating cherry pie in bed. I wipe the crumbs off his pouty bottom lip. That mouth I have already become addicted to admiring never disappoints. If he knew how often just the look of him thrills me, he might be concerned. I'm not entirely sure he wouldn't run from the crazed woman consumed with passion. Here's the thing though. It's not just the physical kind. There's emotional desire and fulfillment that reaches for higher ground. But I could be alone in that conclusion. So I'll keep it to myself.

"Does Maudie ever sleep with you?"

"No. But sometimes I sleep with her."

"Explain."

"Right from the start she preferred her own bed. Downstairs, in front of the big window in the family room. Originally, I put it up here, but she couldn't see out the window. I'd find her downstairs every morning."

"That's so cool. That she wants to look outside."

"You don't know the real Maudie. In her prime she was active and so smart. Independent. She'd take a run at the field and it was really a joy to watch. She's a hound, so the outdoors is where she's in her element."

"Tell me about sleeping with her."

"When she's had a particularly bad day I sleep downstairs on the couch. That way I can help if she needs me."

"Well then let's sleep downstairs tonight. She needs us, right?"

"You'd be willing to do that?"

"Of course. It will be like a slumber party. Just the three of us."

I see his eyes glisten. He reaches out and touches my leg. Then just as quickly changes the subject.

"Have you had enough to eat? I have more pie. And I have ice cream. Vanilla."

I press my lips to his as answer. As far as I can see, this reality I have just been introduced to is a kind of heaven. Sharing ourselves in a deep, meaningful way. It's not just the sex that translates into satisfaction. It's getting to know the other person. What wounds them along with what pleases. The smile that appears on his face matches mine.

"Let me get rid of this," he says, picking up the tray and carrying it to the small round table across the room.

"This bedroom is really big," I add, looking around. "And the bathroom! I've never seen such a great space. You'd laugh if you saw mine."

A sly smile appears on Nobel's face as he rejoins me.

Scooting against the headboard, he threads his fingers behind his head and stares.

"What?" I say.

"Don't pretend you've never been here." He smirks.

Uh oh. When caught deny. Deny. DENY.

"What do you mean?"

"You've been in my bedroom before. I'd guess you were in the bathroom too. Am I right?"

He dips his chin and lifts his lids. "I *never* leave the medicine cabinet open."

Oh fuckity fuck shit. I didn't close the cabinet! Heat rises on my cheeks. But for a moment words are stuck deep in my throat. Think of something!

"I've got cameras. Mostly downstairs, but one is in the hall outside the bedroom. I watched the security clip. Nice work, Dove. You move fast."

He chuckles, and I cover my face with a pillow and scream.

"I'm impressed with your stealthy ways."

The pillow comes down. "I was looking for the Yellow-Tailed Warbler."

I start laughing at my own joke and he joins me.

"Yeah, the ground I'm standing on is pretty shaky."

"That's right!" I roll on top of him. "You stuck your nose in my business first. I would never have done it if you hadn't crossed that line!"

"That's it? No remorse? No apology?"

"You started it." I cross my arms in fake defiance.

A deep sigh escapes as he rolls me off, stands and faces me. Very slowly, he pushes the boxer briefs off and steps out. His cock twitches.

"As your attorney, I'm afraid I have to advise you you're going to be punished for your transgressions."

"If you're my attorney why are you in charge of my

punishment?"

"Because it will please me. Please remove your robe and come lay over my lap. Do it now."

Taking a seat on the edge of the bed, he locks eyes with me.

Oh my. Embarrassment for being busted turns to pleasure. I lose the robe and stand before him wearing just a red thong and matching bra. He bites his lip and chews. I don't think he even realizes he's doing it.

"Please forgive me, sir. It won't happen again," I say, sliding over his lap, ass in the air.

Complete silence as I stare at the door across the room. I look back.

"Am I in the right position?"

A warm hand slides over my cheeks, sending chills up my spine.

His voice is low and soft as he says, "For now."

A sharp sting hits its mark.

"Oh!"

"That's for entering the inner sanctum without me."

"I'm not sorry," I say defiantly.

Another spank. "Ow!"

He leans close to my ear. "Too hard?"

"No," I whisper.

He resumes the play, sliding a finger under the strip of fabric between my cheeks. It's pulled back and he plays.

In a low slow tone, he says, "Your lack of remorse calls for further action. These need to come off."

"If you're forcing me."

"And this bra too," he says, unhooking it like a boss.

I stand and with maddening slowness drop the bra and peel off the thong. I let him have a good long look. Then I lick the tip of my middle finger and place it on my button.

Small circles around and around. As I'm pleasuring myself I'm pleading my imaginary case.

"I've reconsidered my actions of the stated crime. I am really remorseful," I say, never lifting my finger from my clit. It is getting hard not to react to the pleasure. Lady boner.

His jaw clenches. "Come here." He spreads his legs for me to stand between them in my nakedness.

"Your apology comes too late. Now you have to suffer the consequence."

But no slap meets skin. Instead, he presses his mouth to my pussy. Hands wrap around my ass and rub the spot that previously felt the sting.

Then I feel my cheeks part and a finger run up and down to my lips. God. His mouth.

The play continues until I feel the wetness of desire. He dips a finger in the slick juices then licks it off. With one quick movement he picks me up and places me on the bed.

"Show me."

I scoot back against the headboard and pillows and spread my legs. His face transforms.

My fingers part my lips and I squeeze my clit from its hiding place. When it pops out Nobel's breathing changes. His chest rises and falls. He takes ahold of his cock. Stroking it with a steady beat, eyes on my pussy. Lips part and the muscle in his jaw tightens.

As for me, my little pussy is on fire. Already, I am hooked on his sweet man honey. It is my new drug. Not one that will end up taking from me, but one that only knows how to give. The charge I get is thrilling. And it's not just my pussy that reaches the conclusion. It is my heart and mind that arrives at the same time.

With open arms, I look into his expressive eyes. "Come touch me."

Climbing onto the bed he takes me in an embrace. For a moment there is just a look. It speaks of feelings that want to be voiced. Then a hand reaches under my hair and settles on my neck. He takes the kiss. It is gentle at first. But it pushes over the last barrier. We feed on each other's mouth, necks. Ears. Shoulders. My nipples harden with the nearness of his touch. There is no stopping our aim to know each other's body. The feel of his skin, the hardness of his biceps. The roundness of his ass.

I want him closer still. I climb on top and rest myself on his rock hard cock. His hands taking either side of my waist. His hips lifting, feeling the sensation of pussy rubbing back and forth against him in a slow and steady rhythm. There's this sound he makes like a dragon puffing his exhale. My pussy lips surround the shaft. Strong hands feel the shape of me, the sensation of my breasts, the softness of my hands. His eyes close and he leans hard against the pillow taking it all.

When I rise he lifts his cock against my lips, parting them for entry. Taking it slow, I settle onto the rock hardness. Inch by inch, taking the impressive size of him.

"Oh…" Passion grabs the rest of the sentence and throws it against the wall.

But his eyes. They make the stars look dull. They hold me in their gaze and speak of greater truths. I swear he feels it too. In this moment we are one. Movement, breath, heartstrings. The heat builds. And now a beat I haven't known before. It's not just physical. It's the rhythm of two hearts beating as one.

I start to come first. My fingers tightly laced with his. He takes my passion and makes it his own. And as the feeling in him rises to join mine, we soar beyond earthly bounds. And here we are in heaven.

7
Nobel

Only another couple of miles. I reposition the bouquet resting on the passenger seat, so the blossoms won't be smashed against the leather. This is the first time I'm bringing her flowers. And the first I have understood the meaning and beauty of the gift. The Beast is offering the most delicate of gifts for his Beauty.

It would not have been right to bring anything other than her favorite pink peonies. Dove needs to know I listen. My father taught me years ago how important it is in a relationship. I was about twenty-five. It was at my parents' anniversary party and he and I were having cigars and whiskey late into the night. I asked what the secret to his good marriage was. I remember the sureness he spoke with.

He leaned in and said, 'Son, right from the start I listened every time your mother told me something about herself. I paid attention to the little gems she dropped because that's how two people get close."

He took a drag from the Havana.

"That's it?" I asked.

"You need to know each other as you are. You want a

woman to fall in love with the real man. Warts and all. And you want to love the woman she most genuinely is in return, because that is the happy one."

My young self had never thought about it like that. I remember calling him a genius. He laughed at my conclusion.

"Nobody ever really wants to change. You will end up resenting the woman who tries to make you into a different man. Then you'll hate yourself for going along with the idea. We need to be loved as ourselves. That's the secret. Remember that.'

Now, for the first time, the lesson is being applied. Have I ever really thought that deeply about love since that night? It's almost laughable to raise the question. The unequivocal answer is no. In fact, I may have never thought about the conversation again. Till now. But it was there deep inside my subconscious. And now, I have come to understand something I hadn't before. Dove and I reach for higher ground. Even at the beginning. Hope it's real.

Week six into our relationship has arrived, and it's weird I counted. Things are morphing. I've always been consumed by my career. After Kristen's death even more so. But lately, since Dove's arrival, work and most other routines have to be squeezed in among the really important things in life. Like fucking. Or hiking the property and watching Netflix with her. It's strange to have priorities realign. Friends, family, and every other consistency have taken a backseat.

I don't want to be a prick. But shit, I want to concentrate on what calls me. It's not like there is a choice. When I saw my family more happy for me than mad about missing my company, it meant something. They all get it. Every one of them.

Laughing, preparing meals, taking a shower, everything common and normal holds greater weight. Colors are sharper, music more meaningful. And nobody is invited to join our club. Stay away! A memory of the Lyon boys' treehouse with a sign *No Girls Allowed* briefly pops in my mind. I'm changing the rules. This time it reads *Only One Girl Allowed.* One perfect one.

Today brings something new. Meeting the best friend. That, and having lunch at Casa Dove. It will be the first time seeing inside. Not that I have avoided it, but it's just so comfortable at my place. Wonder what kind of taste she has? There has been one clue. Apparently, she's sentimental about her grandparents' things and her home reflects that. She said it one day when we were talking about my taste. She had made a comment that all my heart was hanging on one wall in the kitchen. The pictures. Can't argue with that. Why have stuff spread all over?

Maybe her place will be something completely different from mine. I don't give a damn, except for the story it will tell. I have a feeling we will align despite any differences, making coming together in the future seamless. It only makes sense when everything else fits like a glove.

Things have gone smoothly for us. So far. *Don't get ahead of yourself.* The mantra replays in my head at least once a day as it regularly comes up against my eagerness. Never has the future been on my mind so much. Sometimes life climbs into your bones.

Not being able to spend the night away from Maudie has unexpectedly worked in my favor. There is no need to explain my idiosyncrasies. I like my bed. I feel strange using other people's beds and toilets. How am I supposed to take a shit in an unfamiliar bathroom? The thought makes me cringe. Those are things she'll eventually learn. I could write a book on my habits.

Can't help myself. Even as a kid, it was like that. I have the perfect excuse right now, because it is true. I can't risk being away from the dog. And it hasn't stopped us from being together or spending every Monday, Tuesday, Wednesday, and Thursday sleeping in my bed.

The weekends suck. She is required to perform and rehearse, rehearse, rehearse. To fine-tune new music she and Jimmy write. Getting her sleep, taking care of personal business, doing whatever she does without my company. It all takes time. She reminded me it takes a lot of effort to be serious artists of their caliber.

There are thousands of talented people willing to put the time in, just waiting to take their place. The fact sounds bitter in my mind. But that is just the initial reaction. Being resentful of her talent and career, so she can be at my beck and call, is a move a lesser man might make. That isn't me. I think she's so talented and everyone else does too. Of course, it requires devotion. The truth is, I am constantly having to keep myself in check and remember what my father told me about knowing the real person. It's better to look at the long game.

As I approach the final twist in the road, Siri speaks.

"Your destination is ahead in three hundred feet."

Looking around I take in the houses. Okay, 3607 Cloud Way is next. As I make the turn Dove's home comes into view, surrounded by tall trees standing guard. It's Hansel and Gretel's place, a tiny, enchanted cottage, set back from the street. Looks like it's about to come to life. Bibbidi bobbidi boo, as my mother likes to say whenever she sees something with a Disney quality. The unstructured front yard is flush with wildflowers and rose bushes on one side and a vegetable garden on the other. Colorful stone pathways snake through.

Her two thousand ten Accord is parked on the gravel driveway, in front of a well-restored VW Bus from the sixties. Must be the girlfriend's. Is that music I hear coming from inside the house? Pulling up, I park and grab the flowers. Once out, my question is answered. Definitely music. It's great, whoever is singing. Think it's Sting. A smooth voiced female accompanies him in a soulful jazzy ballad.

Walking down the path leading to the front door, I hear laughter. Male laughter. What the fuck? Who's here? *Calm down.* I really hate this jealousy shit I'm noticing about myself. It surprises me more than anything. Who is this guy I am turning into?

The front door is wide open and Dove comes out dancing barefoot. The sexy beat of the song sets a seductive rhythm, and she knows how to take advantage. Moving with erotic intent, her eyes locked on mine, she sings every word. I have got to remember to add this to our playlist. A pair of low slung green cargo pants hug her waist as hips roll. The short yellow top that stops right under her breasts just about begs me to reach underneath. Shoulder sweeping earrings brush against golden skin. I would like to lay her down between the roses and radishes and fuck her senseless. Instead, I hold out the bouquet.

"Are those for me?" She pretends innocence with a tilt of her head.

"Yeah babe. Come get 'em." Now it's my turn to tease. I lower the flowers in front of my crotch, erasing earlier lofty thoughts about the gift of flowers. Lately my fourteen-year-old boy's sense of humor has made a return. Dove doesn't seem to mind. Instead, she joins in the play. With a sprint, she comes to me and takes the bouquet. I feel fingers wave over my dick. A big smile puts a cherry on the sundae.

Our lips meet under the Montana sun and we share one perfect kiss. I'm about to go for seconds when we are joined by a tall, blue-haired woman standing in the doorway. The expression is of a pissed off babysitter, overwhelmed by the screaming toddlers.

"Excuse me! Hate to interrupt. Dove you better get your

ass in here. I think today's science experiment is about to boil over. Want me to shut the fire off?"

A barely there smile cracks, and a hand raises in a wave, as I hold Dove in my arms. I return the gesture. Dove untangles herself and turns to her friend.

"Deborah, this is Nobel. Nobel, meet our manager, and my best friend forever and ever."

I move toward the woman who is deciding if I pass the litmus test.

"Hi. Nice to meet you."

Instead of a greeting I get a review and a warning.

"Handsome. Hope you aren't too particular about what constitutes a lunch. Or how it tastes. Other than that, it should work out. So, welcome to Casa Dove's Don't Expect Too Much or You'll Be Disappointed Lunch. It's an annual event."

What? I'm not sure how to take the news. But it delights Dove, who does not deny the words and thinks her BFF is funny. "Quit exaggerating! I cook more than once a year!" She says it with no conviction.

As we make it to the door, I get a look from the friend that says, 'You'll see.'

"Give me the flowers, I'll find a vase."

Dove hands over the bouquet and Deborah disappears into the house.

"Your house is really unusual looking, love the garden," I say one second before entering crazy town.

I thought there would be a story, and a quick scan tells one. There's hardly a free space on the walls. Not for one more picture, poster, drawing, or sculpture. It looks like the sixties threw up in here, then came back and got sick again. The only thing I like is the oil painting of Dove. Her face is half in shade, as she sits under a tree. But the eyes. The artist got it right. It goes from the sublime to the ridiculous. Is that a photograph of two old naked people in a hot tub smoking weed?

I don't know where to look first. Yes I do. Tony sits on a purple print couch, strumming his guitar.

"Hey man," he offers, hardly looking away from the strings.

"Nobel, check out the photographs on the wall of my grandparents! And you guys, introduce yourselves! I'm going to attend to the feast."

She heads for the next room, which I think is the kitchen. A giant plant with Christmas lights hanging randomly from the branches covers most of the doorway.

Tony looks up and gives me a smile that the female fans must get off on. I think it's overkill and slightly fake, but girls might like it.

"I'm Tony. Surprised you made it this far, man, most don't. Except for me of course. I have an all access pass." He laughs. He fucking laughed. That was a deep dig. And there is no hesitation letting the prick know how I feel.

"You either just insulted me or Dove or both. Don't do it again."

The genuine surprise on his face makes me question my interpretation of the comment. Shit.

His palm comes up, putting a stop to any further response.

"Dude! I only meant this fucking house is usually much worse than it is today. It's not always easy to navigate through all the instruments or fishing gear, whatever. That's all. She straightened things up for your arrival."

I would be happy to melt into the floorboards. To disappear like a bird in a magic trick. Fuck! I look like a man with zero confidence. Not how I wanted to come across the first time meeting the band.

Deborah speaks up. "You have to forgive my brother. He's going through an emotional crisis."

"Fair point," he says, going back to the guitar. And then as a sidebar, "That may be the truest thing anyone has said to me in years."

I've been in the house for thirty seconds and I'm completely confused. Deborah sees it on my face and lets me in in the private joke.

"He just broke up with his boyfriend."

Oh boy. Did I get that one wrong. Suddenly I like this Tony guy a lot better. His interest in my woman is strictly platonic. It wasn't a jab he threw at me. It was a compliment.

"Don't talk about that asshole. I'm over him," he says.

"Who's the asshole today?"

The keyboardist I saw that first night walks in from the hallway and makes eye contact with me. He moves forward, hand extended. Now this guy has some smarts.

"Hi. I'm Jimmy."

"Nobel."

"Good to finally meet 'the guy.'" His air quotes are questionable. Then he points and the smile fades. "Treat her right. There's four of us watching."

What the fuck? I'm forty-three years old, guy. Is that jealousy behind his eyes? Could be I'm imagining false attacks again. Rivals that do not exist. Calm down, Nobel. You already made yourself look like an ass once today.

"No problem," I say. "It's not my style to do otherwise."

A nod is all I get in response, as he settles next to Tony on the couch. His eyes don't look away from me though. And I saw Deborah shoot him a look. Like she was telling him to back off. For some reason he takes the hint.

"My brother and Jimmy are very protective of Dove. They all are. It's totally annoying most of the time," she says with a dry delivery.

Tony plays a waa waa on the guitar and it makes me chuckle.

So Tony is her brother. Okay. Putting the puzzle together piece by piece.

"Lunch is ready! Everybody grab a bowl, help yourselves, and let's take it out back. There're plates for our bread and salad on the table," Dove calls.

"Sounds good," Tony says, getting up and putting the guitar down.

"It's such a pretty day. Has everyone met?"

Dove's return could not have been better timed. This room and the company need to be aired out. Outside sounds great.

"They met all right. How do you think it went?" Deborah's sarcasm hits the mark.

Dove points a finger in the keyboardist's direction. "Play nice."

So, she identified who would have a problem with me. Why him? Interesting.

"Come on. Jimmy open the wine, will you?"

I follow her into the kitchen and come up against the latest in the day's revelations. It's a small space with a cat sitting on the table, grooming itself. There's a big pot on the stove and what is in it is unidentifiable at this point. But it's red and boiling.

"Get a bowl of my infamous chili," Dove says.

Aha. Chili.

"Get your cat off the table!" Jimmy commands Tony. "That is unsanitary!"

I guess he's not all bad. The cat and his human completely ignore the order. Instead, Tony gives one of his own.

"Pussy, ignore the haters. What's a little cat hair between friends?"

"Pussy is shedding like a motherfucker! I'm putting her down!" Jimmy takes the reins and does what he said.

"What the hell crawled up your ass?" Tony says, scooping a bowl of chili.

I head outside as quickly as possible, mindful of the fact I'm on Jimmy's team as far as the cat goes. There's no reason to divulge that information. I don't have a dog or cat in this fight. I'm playing the guest and don't think anyone has figured out I hate animals around food prep. When Pussy licked herself in the nether regions while sitting on her table throne, I had to look away. It was puke worthy.

Only Dove knows my ways. No one else knows I'm pretty much a minimalist when it comes to décor, or that there's something about order I like. This first look at Dove's habitat is a shocker. I sound like the fucking tight ass I have turned into.

The backyard puts on a show before we make it outside. This time it's a good one. French doors open to a different scene than I expected. Thought there would be more of the same as the front. Maybe more vegetables in the sunlight. Instead, it's all about the natural beauty of the shady setting. There's one wind chime and pots of flowers, but they are the only extras. No garden elves to be seen, not a gnome in sight.

The American Sycamore trees lift to the sky and surround the large patio. You could get fifty people out here comfortably. At least fifty. It is wider than the house. A round ten person table, with a blue umbrella, takes center stage. The patio full of loungers and chairs take up the rest.

"Wow. This is great," I say, trying not to sound surprised.

"It's where we hang out in the spring and summer. You like it?" Dove asks.

"I love it. Great place for a party."

"We have had some outstanding ones. Remember your grandmother's birthday?" Deborah says.

"Oh God! Don't remind me!" Dove chuckles.

As we take our seats, Tony adds his two cents. "The best one was when we all got soused and did the fucked up line dancing. That was *your* birthday, Deborah."

"No," Jimmy says.

With that one syllable word, the table quiets.

Deborah pops back in. "That was a different night."

What just happened? Seems like they all came to the realization of something at once. Except for me. Dove's eyebrow raises slightly, but I see it. She keeps her head down and her spoon in play. Just as Deborah's about to say something, Jimmy interrupts.

"It was the engagement party," he says, looking in my direction. "Dove's and mine."

8
Dove

"I looked like an ass! Why didn't you tell me? It's ridiculous!" Nobel says.

He is pissed off and does not care to hide the fact. The meet and greet ended early and people couldn't wait to get the hell out. That's not a first, which is the point. Unfortunately, he doesn't know why it happened once before.

"I didn't think it would come up so soon! You are overreacting! Let me explain!"

I'm trying to hold my emotions in check, but they are about to boil over. I'm either going to cry or scream. I might tell him to calm the fuck down. Probably the last one.

"Overreacting? You think I don't have the right to expect you to at least warn me when I'm going to be in the close company of someone you have loved?"

He takes a few beats before adding with emphasis, "Or fucked."

The heat rises on my face. "Ohhh. There it is." I point right at him. "That's what this is all about."

He stops and looks me in the eyes. His demeanor calms. Like the eye of a storm.

"No. It isn't. But it's part of it. You were being disrespectful to me hiding something so important to know. It makes it a secret between you two. I don't like that you did that. I have to go."

I feel tears well. He doesn't look me in the face as he moves to the door. It slams in a final statement. I don't think he realizes how hurt I feel. We have only known each other for a short time. I am not required to tell this man every single thing I've gone through. He has nothing to worry about but didn't give me the chance to say.

Closing my eyes, I try seeing things from Nobel's point of view. Once I do it's kind of hard to deny he has a point. Shit. Grandma used to tell me I was my own worst enemy because of my iron stubbornness. Thought I outgrew it.

I figured I had more time to ease into the conversation. Now he is going to think my avoidance equals repressed feelings. How do I explain without sounding pathetic? Or cruel. Or revealing Jimmy's vulnerability. And will he believe me? I can hear him now, pointing out nobody agrees to a marriage proposal unless they want to. Least of all me. Things aren't always black and white. I have to talk with him tonight. In person. Make him understand exactly how I feel about any other man, past or future.

It's dusk when I finally make it to his place. The deep purple streaked sky reflects the mood of the moment. I climb the steps of the porch and feel my stomach turn. There are more than butterflies taking flight. There are condors. I didn't want him to reject my plan to talk it out, so the visit is unannounced. He hasn't called me once since walking out this afternoon. Don't really blame him. Damn.

Remembering the feeling I had when first I saw the view from this porch is the best support I can call on. The feeling of being in a place that means something big in my life. Something true. That could not have been false. Now, I need to put action to feeling. If we are meant to be together, there needs to be clarity about who we are. Right from the start.

He should know the people in my life have been chosen carefully. They are each there by reason of their goodness. I can't imagine life without their friendships. Nobel doesn't seem to have many close friends, other than his brothers. He said it was always like that. And that's okay. For him. I'm a different beast. I like people around me.

I ring the bell and wait. Maudie shows up first, peeking out the window. I wave and make kissing sounds. A wagging tail says her hellos. It feels like a lifetime before the sound of the human's footsteps reach the door. It swings open. For a moment we just look at each other. Then my confidence evaporates, and the tears start streaming.

He takes me in his arms.

"I'm sorry I didn't tell you. I didn't mean to deceive or hide anything," I say, burying my face in his chest. "You have to believe me."

It takes a moment before he responds. When I look up into his beautiful eyes, the anger is gone. But he's still uncomfortable. I can see.

"Let's go inside. We can talk it out there."

Maudie stands guard at the doorstep, and she's watching us. Her eyes are mostly on Nobel and she questions the mood. *Are you sad?* In an offering of love, she licks his hand.

He pats her head. "It's all right, old girl."

I would bet she has been comforting him since returning from my house. It's a dog's love language.

We go to the couch and settle next to each other. Maudie curls at his feet, not wanting to be apart.

"So tell me. When was this and why did it end? I need to know, and then it will never be brought up again."

"That's fair. It was about a year ago."

He doesn't like that, I can tell. Hands comb through his thick hair and rest behind his head.

"So it basically just happened," he says coolly.

"No. Well, yes, but there's extenuating circumstances. Hear me out."

He's silent, staring straight ahead. So I begin.

"Jimmy and I have known each other since we were about nineteen. He's always been in love with me."

"Oh that's great news," Nobel says dryly. "I feel much better."

"Hear me out. I realized it wouldn't be kind to encourage what I did not feel. So, I talked about my boyfriends. I made sure he knew there was nothing but the undying affection of friendship between us. He and I had started a band way back then. Not the one you see now, but the seed was planted. We began writing our own music. We've been together through each incarnation of Montana."

"How did you get from there to an engagement?"

I sigh into the memories of the story.

"My grandmother got sick first. Grandpa and I took care of her for just a year, but it took a toll. For him it was physical. For me, it affected my music. My focus on music and the band had to take second place status. That was just a fact. We lost our bass player and eventually the drummer. Why would talent hang around someone who is not putting the music first? Tony had an offer for another band and had to take it to survive. But Jimmy never budged. He stayed steady with me. Stayed even when his own source of income slid."

Nobel's arms come down and he angles his body toward mine as he listens.

"Then when Grandpa got sick two years later, there was just me to take the mantle. There was no other person to care for him as he deserved. So again, I became a caretaker. I'm not complaining, just explaining."

"How did you survive financially?"

A little snort escapes me. "We had a home, a vegetable garden, and grandpa's social security check to help us. There was a small savings account but that went fairly quick. I had to pick up gigs whenever I could. But by then we had been joined by Oscar and ZZ. They were the best we'd had. I think they could see the writing on the wall because grandpa was already in hospice. It wouldn't be long until we'd be able to concentrate on getting dates booked. They were willing to wait. At the end, Tony came back. And that's what happened."

"I still haven't heard how you ended up engaged to a man you say you didn't love."

"That's the thing. It happened suddenly and I was trapped. Let me explain, please. Just listen."

He remains silent.

"So, all those years, through all the romantic connections for each of us, nothing changed his mind. I could see the longing in his eyes. But he never acted on it. He had always been the most wonderful friend. When my grandparents got sick, he would do whatever he could to help them and me. They loved him. I had no one else to cry to and complain to and just generally let see the rawness of the situation. That's where I made my mistake. I relied on him emotionally. Too much. But in my defense, I was in a fucking storm and I grabbed the lifeboat of friendship. I didn't see that he was mistaking it for a possibility of love. It was entirely my fault, but I was so beat, so wounded, I let my guard down. He mistook my gratefulness as affection."

"Still confused."

"Here's what happened. After my grandfather died, I took a month to decompress. Then I decided to have a party inviting only the closest people to me, the ones who had supported me and loved me so genuinely during the bad years. It was really beautiful, with laughter and tears. Stories. Almost everyone spoke of the love and devotion my grandparents and I shared. We had large amounts of tequila. There was dancing and singing. But around midnight, right in the middle of one of my songs, Jimmy grabbed the microphone. He asked everyone to stop. He took my hand and knelt in front of me. He proposed."

Nobel waits.

"I was so shocked and so was everyone else. But there he was laying his heart out in front of God and friends. The entire world stopped for me as I tried to figure out what to do. The only thing that I could come up with was, say yes. Say yes here, and then I would tell him it couldn't possibly be when we were alone. He could blame the proposal on being drunk off his ass. I could blame my agreement on the same. And that's how it went down."

He sits with the information, absorbing the truth.

"That must have been brutal."

"It was for both of us."

"So you never had sex with him?"

"No. God no."

"He still loves you. Anyone can see it."

I don't contradict the man. I'm not about to start lying now.

9
Nobel

The sound of moving water over smooth stones reaches through the trees. It grows louder with each step closer.

"Watch yourself here," I say, extending a hand.

Who am I kidding? I'd trip over the fallen sapling before she would. Wouldn't be surprised if she leaped over it and did a pirouette. Instead, she goes along with the offer, and takes my hand.

"We're almost there. Just down one more slope."

Passing through the Ponderosa Pines and Sycamores, we head to the river. Before long it comes onto view. A few steps, slope to shore, and we are on flat land.

The last time I was here my ankle was screaming, I was leaning on a rifle crutch and my mind was on the mountain girl I had just risked life and limb to see. The scenery has changed. Were the leaves always this varied in color? Did the scent of the Pines smell so wonderful? It's like that with Dove. My view of the world around and within has changed with her effect.

"Let's go to the fishing hole. I think they would like a good view of the river."

THE RIVER IN SPRING

She adjusts her backpack, and the precious cargo it holds. As we walk, silence accompanies steps. I'm following her lead and respecting the solemn occasion. I never asked when the scattering of ashes would take place. Figured she would know when the time was right and let me know.

Last night in bed I saw her making a list and when I asked what for, she said, "I think I should take Grandpa and Grandma to the river tomorrow. I want to say something that honors them. Just making a few notes."

My nod and kiss on her shoulder was agreement. Anything else would have been intrusive.

It only takes five minutes to reach the spot she has chosen for the final resting place. Light on the water sparkles like newly cut diamonds in the midday sun. The birds are singing an accompaniment, and a fat squirrel runs away between two rocks. There's movement in the bushes. A rabbit appears and watches. Nature is gathering as witness.

"Here," she says. "Let's look for a spot."

"Are you going to scatter on the incline, overlooking the river? Or on the shore?"

She thinks for a few moments before answering. Tears well in her beautiful brown eyes.

"Either way, they will become something new. Part of something else. Wind will blow them against the stones, or water will claim them as part of the river."

As soon as the words leave her lips, she knows what to do. A look comes over her face as if she is a hundred percent certain.

"The edge of the river. That way they'll be here forever and I will be able to be part of where they rest. Oh, Nobel."

The last words soften and are lost on the breeze as she begins to cry. I take our backpacks off and hold her in my arms, kissing the top of her head.

"It's all right babe. This is the perfect spot. Nothing is dead here."

She looks up. "It's so much better than a cemetery, right?"

"Listen to the songbirds. Your grandparents will be in good company."

"Yes. This is the right place. Besides, Grandma always wished she could have seen this spot. Now she will. They used to fish together when she was younger."

"You ready?"

"Yep."

We take the two small urns from our backpacks. I hand mine to her.

"Want me to stay here?" I ask. "I can give you some privacy."

With a shake of her head, she invites me into the intimate moment.

I follow her along the shore to where she had been camped that day we met. Right where the water deepens, and the trout have found their home.

"Here. I want to say something first."

Facing the river, she speaks through her tears. As she begins, a hawk glides over the scene.

"Today you begin your final earthly adventure together, Grandma and Grandpa. You have to go on ahead of me. That's all this is, nothing more. I know we will be together again. Thank you for my beautiful life. You created a happy home and a happy child. You taught me how to care. How to have faith in a Creator and in myself. Thank you for every sacrifice you made. There was big love between us three, and you made sure I knew to always look for it in life and not to settle for less than the real thing. How effortless you made it all seem. You are my heart."

Tears fall freely now, and she wipes them on her shoulders. I allow mine to fall.

"So, I scatter your ashes at the edge of the Yellowstone, under the big Montana sky. The lapping waters will carry you together toward another shore. A more perfect one. A little bit of you will stay here amidst the stones, so I can come talk with you any time I want."

Her head hangs and her voice breaks. "I can't let you go completely. I will love you forever and promise to carry your legacy, your love, and your light as long as I live. Until I see you in heaven, you'll be my sunshine."

Dove hands the silver urn to me and takes the gold one in her hands. She unscrews the lid and holds it to her breast for just a few seconds. Then she tilts the jar close to the shore and gently pours the ashes. When that one is empty, I hand her the second. She does the same, mingling the remains one atop the other. A fine mist of ashes picked up by the gentle breeze lifts and floats into the air.

"See," Dove says, watching the dispersing cloud. "Godspeed."

And then she begins to sing "Calling All Angels". The beautiful voice, breaking with emotion, rises. It follows the now faint cloud. Her love sent as companion to the untethered spirits.

She takes my hand, and we walk. The trip back is taken in silence. Just two people walking each other home. I kind of think being able to be quiet with someone is a greater indicator of a connection than being able to converse.

Walking into the clearing from the trees, my cell sounds. Van.

"What's up?"

"We're here to meet the girl."

Ahead I see Aargons' truck parked on the side of the house. Two figures sit on the tailgate. I'm surprised it took this long. They have no idea what we were doing at the river, so I can't fault the timing.

I look at Dove and cover the speaker. "My brothers are here. Should I get rid of them?"

She looks at me like I'm crazy. If I'm not mistaken, she's actually happy about the news.

"No! I want to meet them. Do I look all right? Is my nose red?"

"You're good. If you're up for it my parents invited us to dinner tonight. But I understand if it's not the right time. I wasn't even going to tell you."

She leans over, grabs me by the face, kissing me a good one. "It's exactly the right time."

I hang up on Van, knowing he and Aargon see us approaching.

She sprints ahead without me. It passes through my mind how different our personalities are. Dove moves toward the unknown. I, on the other hand, stay firmly planted in the familiar. Immediately my brain begins to absorb the news.

Aargon and Van will love her. Okay this is good. I want her to meet the family. And before Scarlett's wedding next month. This is as good a day as any. I can't keep the girl to myself forever. Can I?

By the time I make it to the house the three of them are laughing.

"Gasses? Your mother named you after gasses? I'm sorry, that's brilliant and twisted all in one!"

"Aargon, and Nobel are, I'm a metal, I think. When your mom is a chemist, anything can happen," Van says.

"We like our names. She made us think it was a cool secret to know. It's our sister Helium who got the short end of the stick," Aargon says with a straight face.

For a few beats Dove isn't sure she just heard right. Then she gets the joke and bursts out laughing.

"She's heard me talk about Scarlett," I add.

"Hey brother. Why have you been keeping this woman to

yourself? She could hang with us. Keep up with the Lyon family circus."

"I was going to introduce you."

"When? You forced us to take things into our own hands," Van says.

"We were really busy," I say smiling.

When I look at Dove she's smiling right along with me.

Van jumps down from the tailgate and Aargon follows. We start for the house.

"Tell me one thing, Dove," Aargon says, climbing the steps. "Has he told you his birthday is this month? He doesn't enjoy the day as much as we think he should. Most of our family celebrates birthdays like national holidays. Except for Nobel. We're trying to change that."

I shoot my brother the evil eye and shake my head. Dove looks as surprised as I thought she would.

"No, he didn't tell me!"

I feel a sharp poke to my arm as we reach the door.

"It didn't come up," I say, letting her pass before me.

Turning, she grabs me by the shirt and brings her face close to mine. "Didn't come up? That's very funny." She looks to my brothers and explains. "*My* birthday is next week! The twelfth. He's been planning it for two weeks. What kind of bullshit is this?!'"I untangle from her hold and pin her hands behind her.

"You might want to rethink your aggressive ways, Princess."

This pleases Aargon and Van immensely. They chuckle like they did when we were kids and our mom would call me out.

"It's Nobel bullshit. Have you two met? He's The Invisible Man," Aargon adds. "Sometimes literally."

I feel her arm link in mine. "Not to me he isn't," she says firmly.

Her comment lands in my heart and in my brothers' minds. Her attitude and confidence are not unlike our mother's. They like it, I can tell.

"Mom and Dad are having everyone for dinner," Aargon says. He looks at Dove. "Can you and Noble make it?"

It's said innocently, but my brother knows exactly what he's doing going directly to her. They don't know I've already beat them to the punch.

"I'd love to meet the people who created this one," she says, pitching her thumb at me.

Endearing herself to the brothers Lyon.

They love her already. So do I.

10
Dove

Pop. Snap.

Nobel keeps cracking his knuckles, while we stand at his parents' door. I have never seen him like this.

"Are you nervous?" I whisper.

"No," he says a little too quickly. "Are you?

"No. I'm excited. Don't worry. I'm sure it's going to be fine." I braid my fingers in his.

A look of hope passes behind his eyes. "Did you see something?"

"No. But I have a good feeling." He wants a vision, but none appears. There is only the confidence I feel.

As the door swings open, we are greeted by a striking looking man. It is obviously Dad, because

French artist sensibilities are on full display. Long grey hair untethered, stacked bracelets, and the top three buttons of the chambray shirt are undone, revealing a chest full of hair. I look for the Uggs Nobel said are his staple. I'm kind of disappointed. Tennis shoes have taken their place.

"Bonjour, Dove! Welcome to our home," arms open wide, he calls me in.

"This is my father, Gaston."

I can feel Nobel relaxing when he sees his father. The tenderness it speaks to is beautiful.

I step into the embrace. Powerful arms surround me. It feels warm inside this affection. It is somehow familiar, like we have known each other for years. Double cheek kisses are exchanged. What is that wonderful scent?

"Bonjour, Gaston! Thank you for having me."

"Come here, my son. Give your Papa a hug."

He pulls Nobel into our circle and he messes his hair like a parent would do to his ten-year-old boy. I'm expecting him to be bothered, but it doesn't happen.

With a wave forward, Gaston calls, "Come in! The whole family is waiting!"

Walking inside, the smell of roast in the oven and freshly baked cookies hits at once. It makes my mouth water.

"Is that Nobel?" a woman's voice carries from the kitchen.

"Yeah, Mom. We're here."

Nobel puts a hand on my back as we follow Gaston into the great room. Happy and expectant faces look at the arriving delegation. Here goes. The first sight at who may become my own family. That's how I feel, although speaking it would be a mistake. Not so soon. Over the years I have learned to keep my conclusions to myself. Let everyone arrive at theirs in time without my input.

"Hello! Oh you're here!" Nobel's mother says, coming around the island. I see who he favors. Their eyes are alike. In fact all three boys look like their mother. She's stunning. Wavy, long grey hair and a chic kind of vibe. Not a hippie one like Grandma. More a rich girl on a yacht in the seventies type.

Walking right up to us, she offers a wide smile. "Hello Dove. I'm Aurora. It's so nice to meet you. Oh, and hello to you too son." She laughs.

Nobel just smiles his response.

"Happy to be meeting you too, Aurora. I'll take a hug," I say without a hint of embarrassment.

She doesn't hesitate to bring me close. I think we recognize something in each other that goes beyond the norm. My man is her child. The one who belongs to me, belongs to her too. Respect.

"Now Nobel, introduce your girl to the family and to our other guest tonight. This is Velvet," she says, gesturing to the couch where Van sits next to a woman that may be a stripper. The name and outfit seem to point that way. I notice the unspoken message Aurora sends to Nobel. Her eyes are one millimeter wider. Body language just said a whole bunch.

Van wears a Cheshire grin. Aargon too. When I look at Nobel there is the same expression. The smile DNA. The Lyon boys are going to have a lot to talk about tomorrow.

"Hi, Velvet. This is my girlfriend, Dove."

I love that he said I'm his girlfriend. It's the first time. Velvet barely reacts. She sits like a bump on a log. No return greeting. There is a little smile though. Is she sucking on something? Then a bubble appears between candied lips and pops before it gets too big.

I jump in first. "Nice to meet you. I guess you and I are in the same club."

"Sweet Cheek's?"

Oh shit. That's a strip joint in Billing's. I know because Oscar and ZZ have been there!

Everyone but Velvet realizes the gaffe. But no one points it out or laughs. But Van has trouble keeping a straight face. She's not sure what other club I might be referring to. Her eyebrows knit together. Van must enjoy exceptionally naive women. Those are the kind he prefers, according to Nobel.

When no one explains the comment to the girl, I do. Maybe she's nervous like Nobel was.

"I just meant both of us are newbies meeting the Lyon family."

Her chin lifts in understanding. "Oh." And then a nod.

Nobel gestures to the couple sitting at the island, champagne flutes in their hands.

"That's my sister, Scarlett and her fiancé, Parish."

They welcome me with their eyes and right away I feel the whisper of a connection. Oh. That was strong.

"Hi," I say. "So nice to meet you. And congratulations."

"Thanks," Parish says.

A chuckle slips from Scarlett. "Welcome. It's good to meet the woman who broke down the castle walls."

Nobel holds back a smile. But he doesn't deny his sister's assessment.

"What can I make you to drink, Dove?" Gaston asks. "Nobel? What about you?"

I point to the bubbly. "Is that champagne I see?"

"We are sampling a few for Scarlett and Parish's wedding. Help us!" Aurora adds.

"I'll take a whiskey," Nobel says, rejecting the lighter stuff without pause.

"Can I have another tequila?" Velvet asks, suddenly animated.

The drinks are poured, and passed to us as we take seats next to the about to be newlyweds.

I raise my glass in their direction. "Here's to love. Yours."

Charlotte is pleased with the gesture and lifts her flute. "Chin chin!"

The champagne testers take a sip and I see a few sour faces. It isn't that bad.

"This one sucks," Van says.

"Should have had the Patron." Velvet's contribution lands with a thud.

Van could not care less. Don't think he's interested in her

palate. I would bet it's the enormous boobs that whet his appetite. For her, it's probably his bedroom skills. Nobel did say fucking was Van's favorite pastime. Maybe she likes him for the same reason he likes her. And why not? They could be perfectly matched.

"Have we met before?" I ask Scarlett. "I recognize both of you from somewhere."

"Yes! I can't believe you'd remember. Parish and I were at one of your performances at McCandy's. We spoke to you after the show. Love your music."

"I thought I'd seen you! And thanks."

Gaston gathers the rejected samples of champagne. "Let's get rid of these. I've got another I think you'll like more."

The evening unfolds like all good gatherings do. Organically. With the ease that comes from a shared happy experience spent with people who like to talk to each other and be together. That's what I notice. It is not love alone that lives within this family. They like each other. Can't get better than that. My family had it too.

About two hours in, when the wedding champagne has been chosen and the dinner eaten, we start the dancing. Gaston and Aurora kick it off. Extending a hand he pulls her into the middle of the room, as Marvin Gaye begins to sing "I Heard It Through The Grapevine". Van and Aargon move the large coffee table to the side, making ample room for the featured dancers.

They come together with a smoothness born of years dancing together. She melts into his arms at first, then he swings her out and the real dance begins. Wow. They can move. Gaston is light on his feet, and the fact he is a big man with a belly doesn't factor in his ability to have great rhythm. They both do.

"Come on, kids!" he says, calling us onto the floor.

Nobel takes my hand but remains sitting. He leans in. "I don't really dance."

I watch Scarlett and Parish leave their seats and join in. Van and Velvet too. Only Aargon stays where he is, and he has an excuse. Nobel watches my face for signs of agreement. But that isn't going to happen.

"Are you injured?"

He is amused by the comment.

"Well, if you see me dance my ego will be bruised."

"Just do it. It's so much fun. I really like to dance. I'll do something I'm uncomfortable with when you ask," I say, pleading my case.

It's an offer I may live to regret, but for now I can't really think of anything he'd want me to do that I would refuse. I'm an adventurous sort. More than he is.

His shoulders sink, but God bless him, he gets up.

"Okay. I'll try. But if I say that's it, please listen."

"Okay, great. I will. This is a good song."

We move to the middle of the dance floor/living room and immediately I see his family watches. But when he notices, they look away. Everyone acts like this is perfectly normal. Only Gaston keeps eye contact and sends an excited thumbs up.

He takes me in his arms, and although it's an upbeat song, he dances slow. I don't say a word. This is step one in a one hundred level journey to becoming comfortable on the dance floor. We sway back and forth. We are slightly offbeat, but no sense pointing it out.

"See! It's not so bad, right? You're doing good!" I lie.

How the hell does a man so adept at lovemaking become so stiff when he tries to get his groove on? Well, if I have to choose one over the other, I know where the choice falls.

"I look like a dork," he whispers in my ear.

"You do not. Just relax. You're holding me and I'm looking

in your eyes. I see nothing but your fabulous face. Can you feel my body swaying with you?"

"I feel your boobs against me and if I bring you any closer, you'll feel my dick. The rocket is waking up. Want to go home and fuck?"

Just as I'm about to answer Van and Velvet pass by. I'm certain they just heard the word fuck, because they both chuckle in our direction.

The song ends and the next one on the Lyon playlist begins. There's no slow dancing to this one. But he holds on tight.

"Okay, now you are going to add your hips to the mix. Put your hands on mine."

He does and I make a slightly exaggerated lift side to side.

"Just like this. You now," I say.

He makes tiny itty-bitty movements in the general direction of mine. When we fall into a synced rhythm he smiles.

"Am I doing it?"

"Yep." I smile at my John Travolta.

"We look nothing like Boom Boom and my brother," he says, nodding in their direction.

If ever there was an uninhibited dancer it's Van. Kind of like a kid with no inhibitions. He's matching Velvet's steps and arm movements. Trying to. It's impossible to match Velvet's professional looking moves as she gets lost in the music. You have got to appreciate the girl's ability. Van is beyond a doubt appreciating it. Alcohol has made an enormous difference in some people's hesitations. Nobel is still up on the dance floor, and that's proof enough.

"Let's go dance by Van!"

I bet that's the first time Nobel said that sentence. I feel his chains weakening.

. . .

It's midnight. We lost Aargon first, then Velvet and Van ten minutes ago. Scarlett and Parrish, and Nobel and I are the stragglers sobering up with coffee and conversation with Gaston and Aurora.

"How did you two meet?" I ask.

"We met on a beach in winter." Parrish takes Scarlett's hand and kisses it. He doesn't let go.

"There wasn't a meet cute for us," Scarlett says.

Something passes between the two of them. A big story that can't be told tonight. That's how I see it anyway.

"I went to Maine to be with Sam, when my sister died."

Oh. Damn.

Aurora weighs in. "When Kristen passed, she and her family were living in Maine. Thankfully, Scarlett was able to relocate there for Sam."

Parrish picks up on the story.

"I was getting through my own issues. Processing grief and loss by hiding in my writing. My son had died some years before. Anyway, we met on Martin's Beach, and the rest is history. Now we are a family. Scarlett, Sam, and I. There's something to be said for destiny. I don't think it can be ignored."

"Don't forget Boo!" Scarlett says.

"That's right. The dog had lost his family too."

I take in the drama of their coming together. It is so different from the story of Nobel and me. Their love story wasn't easy to tell or to live. It must be solid to go through that kind of start and end up here. The pain solidified what they found in each other. I can see it on their faces, and I feel it when they speak.

11

Nobel

Wiping the last traces of shaving cream off my face, I pick up the cell and take Dove off speaker.

"What were you and my mother whispering about on the phone last night?"

The few second pause in her answer confirms something is up.

"What do you mean? We were just talking about having your family come to McCandy's for a show sometime. That would be fun, right?"

"I call bullshit."

That wasn't it. But I have my own secrets and they will be revealed tonight. Hope it goes as planned.

"What?" she says. "You're paranoid. Let's talk about *your* birthday. I want to celebrate it even if you don't," she says, changing the subject.

"Uh huh."

It is an obvious effort to misdirect the conversation.

"Let's get past yours first. Then we can discuss if we need to plan anything. You know what I'd really like?"

"Me naked in your bed?"

"Well yeah, babe. That would be the best birthday celebration you could plan. Let's lock it down."

Her giggles spark my dick to respond.

"Of course, that will be part of your gift. But we need to do something special. I want to. Come on. Please."

There's no refusing her. It isn't in me. There has never been a problem before about doing what the hell I want to do. When I wanted. Before Dove I saw no reason to bend to things that I didn't care to do. You do you, I'll do me. Even stupid things like birthday celebrations. I was that guy. Period. Now, somehow things look different. It is because I am a different man with her. An improved one, most likely.

"Whatever. I guess a nice dinner out would be fine," I give in to logic and kindness.

A little snort precedes her answer. "Okay good. I'll keep it simple."

Do I believe her? Not sure I do. That snort sounded suspiciously like it was hiding a lie. What has she planned? I may regret my recent evolution.

"I'll pick you up at seven tonight," I say, walking into the bedroom. "We can have a few drinks before dinner."

"Where are you taking me?"

"Oh no, you're not getting that information. It's a surprise."

"All right, Mr. Invisible. Wherever you've decided on will be perfect, because we will be together."

"That's right, babe. You and me. That's all we need."

I want to say the words *I love you*, but this isn't the right time. It's coming though. I feel it rising and I don't know if I can stop myself from blurting it out.

Four hours later, we are on the way to the celebration. The clear starry night is a perfect backdrop for the occasion. I glance at Dove, sitting next to me as we drive to the restaurant.

"You look beautiful tonight."

"Thank you, baby. My underwear matches."

"Prove it."

She unbuttons the front of the dress and gives me a peek. Light blue lace bra. Nice. My hand slips beneath the edge of the fabric, and I feel the softness of her skin. As I return my hands to the wheel, she lifts and straightens her skirt.

"What do you think of my hair tonight? Thought you might like to give it a tug later."

She chuckles, but she knows me. I definitely want to pull that hair. Just the thought of leaning her head back gives me a mini-boner. The way the sky-blue dress hugs her body and how her blonde hair is loosely braided over one shoulder. Wow.

She's mowed down every other woman I have ever known. But it's more than what's on the outside. Much more. I'm aware I sound like every cliché ever uttered about men and love and lust. How it becomes all mixed together and takes over a man's mind.

The left clicker sounds, signaling to her where we may be headed. Think she'll figure it out now. Peripherally I see her head pick up.

"Can it be? Are you taking me to Lotus?"

"You mentioned you always wanted to go there."

"But you don't like sushi!"

"It's not about me tonight. You are the birthday girl. Besides, I've decided to expand my palate. I'm going to try it again."

"I love you for doing that," she says, sending an air kiss my way.

Did she just say she loved me? Not really, but it's good enough for me to take it further. I turn into the restaurant's driveway and get in line for the valet before responding. Turning to her, and taking her hand, I lay it out.

"I love you for all kinds of things."

I say it clearly, so it cannot be misinterpreted or dismissed as a sound bite. A smile breaks out on each of our faces as eyes lock. We have been dancing around this moment for weeks. But we need to move to the center of the dance floor, pause and stop everything else.

"You do?"

"I do. I love you, Dove. And if it's too much, I don't care. That's how I feel."

Our fingers braid and I'm loving the look on her face. It's for me alone.

"That's how I feel too. I love you, Nobel. All the way. Oh God. Here we are."

The line of cars moves up. We are next.

"This isn't the most romantic of settings. In a car, at a sushi restaurant." I laugh. "But I couldn't wait another minute to tell you."

Her hand lifts to my cheek. "Wherever you and I are is the right place. We carry it with us now. Everything has changed."

"Everything, love."

In this moment I am flying among the stars. It's just begun, and I wish it would last forever. As if the Universe heard my feeble wish and said "no" her door and mine open at once, breaking the spell.

"Good evening," the valet says unaware of the weight of the moment. Now the world reminds us other people occupy it too. We exchange key for ticket.

"Good evening."

I exit and come around the car. One kiss. Her joy. Mine. Some sort of visceral excitement is going on in my stomach. And there is the feeling of an altered mindset where someone else's welfare and happiness reigns. As soon as I said the three words, it became obvious. It seems as if the reverse is true too. Think she feels as I do. I hold the elevated position in her mind. I have no idea how I know that other than her face looks exactly how I am feeling. So, this is love. It is more than I knew.

The entry door to the restaurant opens and a man lets us pass.

"Welcome to Lotus. Enjoy your night."

"Oh, we will!" Dove says. "It's my birthday! And this guy is in love with me," she teases.

"That is true!" I add.

This delights the man, who sends her a wide smile. And I admit her enthusiasm is catching.

Walking inside, I wait for the group standing ahead of us. They give their name and follow the hostess to be seated. It gives me time to hold Dove close. PDA has never been my thing. Before meeting my mountain girl. Now I barely give it a thought. If I want to touch her, I do. The public is lucky I don't do more. Decency is the only thing holding me back sometimes.

This place is obviously popular. I made the reservations a few weeks ago and didn't get in at first. They called back after a cancellation. Otherwise, my plans would have had to be reworked. Every table seems to be taken. Low lighting and upscale décor set a mood that suits how special this night is for us.

The hostess returns and takes her place at the podium.

"Good evening."

"Lyon. Reservations at seven."

The attractive hostess, dressed as if she stepped out of a designer's fashion show, checks for the name and does exactly as I had requested. She doesn't say anything else about the reservation.

"This way, please."

With a hand on Dove's back, we follow the woman through the room to where a private alcove is waiting. I can't see if everyone is here until we are almost at the entry. Then, when Dove sees she makes a happy sound. A kind of squeak.

"Ohh! What did you do?"

As I round the corner the table comes into view. Good. They all made it.

Dove starts tearing up. "You guys! This is so beautiful!"

"Happy birthday!!" everyone calls to the birthday girl.

A few people raise cocktails or sake cups in honor of their friend. All four band members, their dates, best friend Deborah and hers, and us two make the party of twelve. The large square table is already filled with cocktails and appetizers. I don't mind they started without us. I'm just glad they agreed to show up on time for the surprise.

I wasn't so sure Jimmy would agree to come. The woman beside him is not who I imagined he would bring. Not that I know him at all. But she is older and plainer than expected. He definitely does not have a type.

"Anna! It's so nice to see you!" Dove says it as the woman rises and comes in for a hug.

"You look so pretty!" Anna says.

"Nobel, this is Jimmy's sister, Anna."

"Thanks for joining us, Anna. Nice to meet you."

So, he brought the sister. That's kind of weird. Doesn't the guy know any women he could invite? Maybe he is sending my woman a message. Don't want to think of it now. Dove makes the rounds, kissing each cheek.

"Does everyone know each other? ZZ, Oscar, I don't think you have met Nobel yet." Dove says it as she takes the seat next to mine.

"We talked on the phone," ZZ says dryly. He pours himself some sake. "For at least five minutes."

"How the hell did you get him to talk that long?" Oscar asks me.

That starts off the rest of the friends retelling of infamous ZZ habits. The recluse tendencies, and how he never wants to talk to fans.

'Don't scare my date," he says after a particularly sketchy story.

She isn't scared. I'd say she is having a good night by the smile on her face.

I feel the warmth of Dove's hand as it touches mine. She leans in. "Oh, Nobel. This is wonderful. Thank you, baby."

"I called all of them. Wanted to make sure your celebration would go smoothly. Besides that, I needed to apologize to those who witnessed my reaction at your house that first day I met them."

Dove looks surprised. "You didn't need to do that. Not for me anyway. You don't realize yet what a bunch of fuckups and hotheads they can be. I guarantee every one of them will piss you off soon enough."

"Hey you two. Pay attention to us! This is our time!" Deborah calls.

For emphasis, Tony tosses a piece of sushi at my head. But The Invisible Man learned early to dodge whatever Aargon and Van shot my way. Rocks, dinner rolls, baseballs. Dirty underwear. My lightning reflex deflects the food and sends it to the ground.

At this moment it's painfully obvious I'm dealing with people younger than me. I remember how fun it was. But I notice tonight how my idea of funny has changed. Other things have taken their places. I'm becoming my father. For the first time I realize what a great thing that is. Doesn't mean I'm old. It means I am getting smarter.

Laughter erupts from Deborah. "That was brilliant hand eye coordination, Nobel. You are outmatched, brother."

Tony reaches for the tuna roll. "I have no idea what my sister is talking about," he says to his date.

George, the hot, young, body-builder hasn't said two words. The guy's thick head of dark hair is groomed within an inch of his life. The clothes he wears are tailored perfectly. How did he find a shirt that fit those biceps?

"Did you ever hear about the time Oscar and Tony decided to go skinny dipping in the mayor's pool?"

"That wasn't my doing!" Oscar protests. "He thought the guy was hot and I was just supporting his urges."

When his date's eyes widen, he adds, "You know, like a good friend does."

One funny memory after another is told as we sample massive amounts of sushi and sake. Lucky for us, the owner is here tonight. She recognized Dove and the other members of Montana. She fangirled all over them and suggested we allow her to choose the feast. Deborah took her address to send autographed pictures.

Okay. I had to force myself to partake in some of the slimier looking choices. And it took a few sakes to get me to the sashimi. But they sort of won me over bite by bite. That, or I'm too pickled in alcohol to make any good choices. I'm probably growing a ten inch worm in my intestine right now.

The conversation turns to music. That must happen a lot. Their animated faces wear a version of the expression. There is a look when people speak of what they love. Energy picks up. And it shows in the eyes. I see it here, all around the table.

"I've heard the story how Montana came to be, but what about the future? Do you have long-term plans?"

I ask not only to hear the band's goals, but to solidify in my mind what Dove is reaching for. It will affect me. I expect Deborah to answer. As I take a bite from the elaborate roll, Jimmy does.

"Same as always, brother. We want to make it on the national stage. Eventually international. Write songs. Make records. Tour. World Domination. Nothing has changed."

Message received. You hope I have zero effect on Dove's trajectory. That's how you see it, now let's hear from the only voice I care about. I look at her and wait.

"Well, yes. That's it in a nutshell," Dove says with a pleased look on her face and a lift of her sake cup.

Shit. She agreed, didn't hesitate, or make any adjustments to his narrative. There was not a second thought about Jimmy's conclusions. He looks happy as shit. And for the first time tonight he sends me a smile that's says he knows her better than I do. Fucker.

"That sounds great. I bet you will be on that stage someday. Someday soon."

My words settle on the faces of the people at the table. Maybe some believe me. Others know I'm spouting what they want to hear. Definitely Jimmy does. But another might as well. For different reasons though. Deborah. Her eyes tell me she is looking at the whole picture. Aware of both my good intentions and her friend's feelings toward me. In this moment I understand Dove's choice of best friends.

How I feel is not politically correct, or loving. I know that. But I do not want my woman to be on the road three hundred days out of the year. Or be around fawning male fans who would love getting in her pants. Not to mention being around a man who loves her. The one that isn't me, while I sit at my desk reading legal papers. In my house alone, in the middle of Paradise without my Eve. No man would blame me for feeling this way. But the women, they would not share their opinion. Not even my own mother, who would give me a twenty-minute lecture on the importance of supporting your mate. Not to mention that all men should encourage financial stability in women. Then she'd segue into the history of women supporting the dreams of their men. I don't have a leg to stand on.

But wait. What are the chances of fame ever happening? Am I a huge dick for even thinking that? No. It's just the facts. I know nothing about the music business, but even I know the chances are slim. Talented singers and musicians are everywhere. Most never know success on that level. That is an unvarnished truth in life. It especially applies to the arts.

I wish them well, and know their talent warrants it, but it's a long shot. The odds of Montana reaching the heights they deserve probably will never happen. *So calm the fuck down and show your support.*

Quickly I regroup and put back on a cool persona. Jimmy. What kind of a pussy name is that? Can't let him know he got me good. Obviously, he isn't finished with what he has to say though, because he points in my direction. Round two.

"What about you, Nobel? Dove said you work from home. You're an attorney, right? It's not quite as exciting as making music, but I bet the money is better and steadier," he says, pretending he's making the effort to get to know me.

What is happening is he's pointing out my career is boring and lacking in any excitement whatsoever. I'd say he is attempting to point out to Dove how colorless life would be with a man like me. How dry and dull her days would be. Thing is, he has not considered the most important detail.

"True. The days can get a little routine," I say, looking at Dove and smiling. Then I turn back to Jimmy.

"But the nights? I think those are every bit as exciting as you'd imagine."

Imagine is the operative word, dude. That is what you have to do. I live it. His face begins to flush with my words. You could hear a pin drop. Literally. Three people start talking at once, filling the void. But Jimmy and me? We are both silent.

In reality I'm sure he would much rather grab the back of my head and smash my face into the table. For emphasis. Just as I'd like to do with his. An image of his rather large nose breaking comes to mind. I wouldn't hate it if there was a pool of blood involved.

Get ahold of yourself. Do not show this jealous side or any lack of confidence. I smile before responding.

"Yeah. I'm hired by other attorneys to weigh the evidence of their cases. Sounds boring, but it's far from that. It's heavy on the cerebral."

I pause after that declaration just to make sure he understands the insult. How I am turning his own words against him. I can give as good as he can.

"And yeah, the pay is good," I continue. "And reliable. But then it's not as exciting as a keyboardist's life. That's for sure."

I add a half grin and my tone sounds sincere. That's how good I can fake it when someone deserves nothing less. This is his doing. I am just a player on the stage he built. Hopefully, he hears the message I am sending.

And he does. As the conversations continue and the toasts are made, he's eyeing me. Not with a smile or relaxed body language. Instead, dark eyes and a furrowed brow accompany his silence. Like he's deciding what to do next. Yeah, I don't much like you or your intentions either, guy. I see you.

12
Dove

Come on! It's your birthday. I have plans, you know."

"I just have to finish this one thing," Nobel says for the third time.

I have left him to his work for the last two hours as planned, but soon I'm going to head for the river with or without the man.

"You have five minutes. Tick, tick, tick. We are on a schedule!"

His eyes lift to mine and he smiles and stretches. "All right, warden. Let's go fishing."

Maudie's head turns as Nobel gets up and makes his way to me. Her understanding of the inflections in her human's voice is impressive. Even without us being by the door, she knows we are about to leave the house.

"You look awfully cute, you know. Reminds me of when I saw you that first day. Except for the naked thing."

We come together into default position. Arms encircling bodies. The kissing. The wonderful kisses.

"Happy birthday, baby. I love you."

"This is the first time I've looked forward to the day since I was twelve."

"From this one on, it's going to be your favorite day of the year."

"You're aiming a little high, aren't you? It's just not my thing to be the center of attention."

I spank his ass. "We need to make up for all the ones you missed celebrating. And I know how to win you over."

"You already have. In every other way."

"How did you end up loving a woman who thrives on the spotlight?"

"The law says it's opposites that attract. We balance each other."

"So today, being that it's my choice, I'm going to take you a bit out of your comfort zone."

His arms drop and he takes a step back.

"Wait a minute. Don't go crazy. What have you planned, Dove?"

"Quit worrying. Grab your jacket. You're going to love it all."

"I think that was the headline on the Titanic brochure."

―――――

Nobel watches me pouring mimosas by the river, under the big sky.

"How'd you get all this stuff here without me knowing?"

I point to my temple and wink. "Planning and timing. I started bringing things down two days ago."

"I'm impressed."

"I'm impressed!" I say, watching Nobel fry the freshly caught trout. My compliment is returned with an exaggerated look of disbelief.

"That I can fry a fish?"

"No! That you caught one and then cleaned it like a boss."

"Is there any man or boy, living in Montana, who doesn't have that skill set?"

"Of course there is."

I spread the flowered quilt Grandma made me on a flat space beside the river and place the two big green pillows side by side.

"That's nice," Nobel calls as he removes the pan from the fire.

What a god. I don't think I've ever been more attracted to the man than I am in this moment. He's having more fun than I hoped for. I can tell. Lookin' good in that old jean shirt. It shows off the flat stomach and wide shoulders. Fuck. Good idea. Definitely after lunch. I've got it all planned. If I can make it that long without tackling and mounting him like the animal I am.

"You want this on that plate?"

"That's good. Put it with the other food on the table."

I walk over and take out the potato salad from the cooler. "Go sit on our magic carpet, birthday boy. I've got this. Oh! Take the champagne and glasses please."

He doesn't fight the plan, and I get a kiss as he leaves. Making a plate for myself and one for him, I add one small flower at the edge of each dish.

"You look extra beautiful like that. Barefoot in the kitchen," Nobel calls. "I'm serious."

I take no offense to the compliment. In fact, he gets a happy dance. It isn't meant as a macho cry. He is just saying he loves this part of me too. Not just the glitter, but the glue.

As I hand the plates over and he sets them between us he adds another thought.

"I left one thing out. I think the saying goes 'barefoot and pregnant'. What are your ideas about that?"

The surprise on my face must be obvious because he starts laughing. One open palm comes up before his words.

"No pressure. Just think it's something we should know about each other. Are kids in your plan?"

I take a seat and look him in the eyes. "Eventually. Yes. Definitely. You?"

"To tell the truth, I never put much thought into the idea. That sounds ridiculous for a man my age, but it's fact. And suddenly the subject has popped up occasionally in my mind. It must be the Dove Effect."

My body is tingling with some weird response to the words. I don't know what that means, but I think it's positive. Otherwise, I'm having a stroke.

"Here's the thing, Nobel. I'm at the place in my career that it's either going to happen for me or it isn't. We don't have an infinite amount of time to be discovered. Babies don't factor into my life right now. I have time, reproductive wise. What are your thoughts? Do you think you want to be a father?"

"Yeah. I think I do."

As the words leave his lips a faint image appears. Nobel is sitting on the big boulder a few feet away. His back is to me. A laughing toddler sits on his lap. Sitting next to Nobel is a woman with shoulder length dark hair, wearing a blanket around her shoulders and a hat. She has a hand on the child's head. What? It dissolves before I have a chance to see more, and my heart begins to beat faster.

"Yoo who?" he says, calling me back.

"Sorry. I was just thinking."

"This fish is delicious. I did an excellent job if I don't say so myself. And here's to weak tree branches," he says, lifting his mimosa.

"To weak tree branches and the man who fell for me," I add.

I push the image aside. It doesn't mean anything. She could be a friend. Or a cousin maybe. It could happen. Shit. But I know without doubt that she was feeling love for the child and the man. I could sense it. It seemed to be the most important piece of the puzzle. There is no denying that. No. That was not a glimpse of the future. It's just my paranoia of losing him.

We get to the feast by the river. He is the best company I have ever had. Smart and funny. Romantic. Expressive. There is this sense that I am the only woman who he has opened up to. This is my man. Not the woman with the dark hair. I refuse to bow to the image. We have free will and I will use mine to make our love a lasting reality. I'm getting riled up with the thought of another woman loving him.

He stretches out on the pillow, as I move the dishes off the quilt then join him. A hand comes up to my face and moves a long curl back. His eyes tell a story I want to hear.

"Let's just kiss till we're naked."

"Great idea," I say, taking the first one.

Kissing is grossly underrated by everyone who is not a good kisser. Nobel doesn't fall into that category. He takes his time with each one, until we can feel the passion build. He changes it up, which is one of the secrets. It's soft and deep, then my neck gets the attention. Once in a great while he catches my bottom lip between his teeth. Yes. His tongue is an erotic tool, taking its pleasure and giving it in kind. And how he holds my head in his palms. I love that.

Under the summer sun, we start taking our clothes off. Correction. He starts taking my clothes off first. I feel alive. Shorts unzipped and my T-shirt lifted over my head. I bought a new bra and panties for his birthday fuck. Well, for the first one of the day, anyway.

"Love this," he says, unhooking the see through lavender bra with lace at the edges. "Let's get rid of it."

It goes flying to the ground. He turns me on my back and gets on his knees, stripping off his T-shirt and tossing it aside. He unzips, stands and peels off his jeans. The impressive cock pops up ready for the job ahead. No boxer briefs. He is free-balling it. That just made me wet.

He bends over and peels off my shorts, revealing the matching see through panties. There is a moment where he just looks at my half-naked body. Sunlight highlights the dark tones of his hair and the muscles of his arms and legs. The V leading to his cock is by far the most sensual part of his body. Is he going to remove my last remaining piece of clothing? But he leaves them on. Oh!

Kneeling between my legs his head dips to the honey-pot. I feel his tongue trace the length of my lips. Oh. The fabric of my panties is a little stiff and that works beautifully. It's the right amount of rough over my clit, which is at attention. His teeth grab the panties' edge and pulls it to the side. One hand holds it back as he eats me till I'm moaning.

"Oh my God."

He takes the sides and pulls them down and off. They must be on the ground too, but I'm too excited to bother looking. Nobel resumes the loving. The worship at the altar of my pussy. The climb. Here it comes. Here I come. Here. Here!

"Ohhhh, yes! Yes!"

I start to come. Oh shit! This is going to be great! I can tell whenever the buildup takes this long from the beginning of the orgasm to the first moment of the release. Yes! He licks the juices flowing from my pussy and it takes me to another world. Maybe it is the river or the sun or the fact his mouth and my clit are best friends. It's everything.

I grab ahold of his head. "Stop. Stop. Oh my God!"

His smiling face lifts to mine. There is a thin glisten of my cum all around his mouth. "You really came a lot! That's fucking sexy as hell."

I study his fabulous face while catching my breath. "Now give *me* a taste."

He laughs and rolls to his back. His legs spread wide as I move between them. My hands sweep the skin between his thighs, knees to crotch.

"This is definitely my favorite birthday. Let's do it every year."

Taking his cock in my hands is agreement. I gently kiss the tip then circle the head lightly and slowly with my tongue. I flick the tip and send a charge to his balls.

"Oh," the word escapes in one exhale. His body lifts, shoving his dick to my mouth. I take the unsubtle hint and wrap my lips around the head, licking the hole. Then I start the hand roll, moving up and down with a light but firm grasp. My special move is to squeeze just a little on the backstroke. As I do it, Nobel reacts as expected. It makes him crazy, and he let me know the first time we fucked.

"Babe…yeah, oh yeah…fuck."

Hands reach for my hair and he grabs thick bunches in his fists. Lift and lower, suck and suck and suuuck more. Lips wrapped around the engorged cock. Tongue licking and teasing. He begins to moan and his breathing becomes heavier.

"Ummm. Hummm…. Oh babe. Don't stop. Ohhhhhh fuck!!"

As I start from the base and pull the orgasm to me, I decide not to let go. Come in my mouth, baby. Come. When he realizes I'm not going anywhere he holds my head steady. Here it comes. Mt. Vesuvius erupts. Shit. This is more than I expected! Whoa! I almost start laughing because my gag reflex has been alerted.

I take it all and he pumps till every drop is spent. I lift my head and look for the nearest place to deposit the proof.

"Whoa! That was...that was awesome!" he says, coming up on his elbows.

"Grumphksdh." That was 'glad you like it', with a mouthful of cum.

I grab the nearest cloth napkin I bought for the birthday celebration and put it to good use. I will never look at them in the same light again. Every time I set a table with these I'm going to be transported back to this moment.

As soon as I rid myself of the extra weight of .0002 ounces of Nobel's man nectar, I offer a song.

"Happy birthday to you! Happy birthday to you..."

He starts laughing.

"Happy birthday dear Nobel. Happy birthday to you!"

"That is by far the finest gift I have ever received. Not the song. The blow job. Thank you, babe. You are an impressive woman in more ways than one."

I come up beside him and lightly kiss his penis. The parting message? "Mine."

Part two of the day's itinerary involved a little more planning. But everyone is following instructions. We need to sell the fact it's just another birthday for Nobel. We already celebrated at the river. His family has always respected his wishes for the most part, not making a big deal of the day. There were dinners at Aurora and Gaston's, or barbecues at one of their houses.

But nothing like we are going to have tonight. All through the afternoon Nobel is getting calls and talking to his family as if he won't be seeing them here tonight. The music is playing in honor of the birthday boy. I check the time and calculate the remaining minutes I have till blastoff. Maudie is following me around, as if she understands something is up.

Smart dog. Wait till she sees her friend. I wasn't about to leave Nobel's baby out of the party.

"Stay out of the kitchen!" I yell as Nobel comes down the stairs. "And the guest rooms! Go sit in the living room!"

"God, you're a bossy bitch," he teases.

I get a glimpse of the handsome man dressed for the occasion he believes it is. The occasion being an intimate relaxing dinner for two and a Netflix movie. Poor baby. He thinks I'm paying attention to his crazy rules. That's hysterical. Don't make a big deal of the auspicious day. Let's just have a private celebration. Well, we did that earlier. I can't think of anything more private. So I get credit for that, right? Now it's time for family fun.

"What's cooking? Smells great."

"Don't worry about it. Quit asking questions you're not going to get answers for."

Does he really think I'm cooking anything complicated? My reputation in the kitchen precedes me. I faced it long ago. I'm a bad cook. This fudge is about the most exotic thing I know how to make. Aurora told me that's Nobel's favorite candy, so I claimed it.

"You better be nice to me or I'll go look in the guest rooms. There must be a present hidden there."

Spoon in hand, I peek around the doorway. "I swear to God, if you do that, I'm never going to blow you again."

"Don't be cruel. It's my birthday. And is that chocolate I see on the spoon? Bring it here."

Walking over, I hand him the spoon to lick. "I think it's a great idea to eat dessert first. I do it regularly."

He wraps an arm around me as he makes quick work of the fudge. "I knew I loved you for a reason. What other woman thinks like that?"

"None probably. But why have unnecessary rules?" I take a lick and a chocolate kiss.

The sound of cars approaching and headlights through the windows pulls our attention. Oh, they're here! Nobel's eyes meet mine.

"Are we expecting company?"

I untangle myself from his arms and head for the kitchen.

"We are. Let me get rid of this."

"Dove, what did you do? Am I going to be happy?"

"That's entirely up to you, darling."

He swings the front door open and watches as the Lyon family park and get out of their cars. I join him and link my arm in his. Every person is carrying a covered dish. Thank God they agreed so easily, otherwise it would be take-out. Did Nobel tell them I suck as a cook? I would if I were him. That way I will never be expected to whip up a gourmet meal. A person can't be good at everything. I prefer singing and fucking as opposed to any of the other talents.

"The boys came!" he says, eyeing Sam and Teddy.

I know he is glad they are here. At sixteen it wasn't a given until I enlisted their services. The wide smile on Nobel's face cannot be faked. I knew it would be this way. They are way too joyful a family to be anything other than happy to be celebrating each other.

Ding dong, ding dong, ding dong. Van leaves his finger on the doorbell despite the fact we are standing at the open door.

"The birthday brigade has arrived!" The voice carries over the music as he walks in.

"What did you bring, brother?" Nobel says, eyeing the foil covered casserole dish. "Don't think I know your specialty."

"Yes, you do. I brought Grandma's cold pasta salad."

Nobel lifts the corner of the foil. "I have literally never seen this before. But it looks good."

Van knows he's busted. "Okay maybe I got the recipe from the back of the mayonnaise jar. It was easy. Give a man a break."

He gets a slap on the back. "You're right. I appreciate the effort."

"Thankfully, I will always be a worse cook than any of you, so you are safe," I say, exchanging cheek kisses as he heads for the kitchen.

"Welcome!" I say to the approaching guests. Aurora and Gaston come with a tote bag of goodies as well as two shallow glass dishes of family recipes.

"Hello, darling! Happy birthday!

He gets kisses from both parents.

Aargon carries a large indoor plant.

"A plant in my house?' Nobel says as it passes in front of him.

"Yeah. You need it. Mom said."

"Okay then. I guess I can keep it alive."

"Everyone! Put the food on the kitchen island. We'll serve ourselves from there," I say, being team leader.

Aargon calls to Van. "Hey why didn't you bring the stripper?"

The teenagers find this very amusing. Teddy is nodding like he knows what his father is asking about. Come to think of it he probably does. To the person, they are open with each other. Why would it be any different for father and son?

Van sends a sneer in return. "She isn't a stripper. She just works at a gentlemen's club," he says chuckling. "As an interpretive dancer."

"And so what if she is?" I add, sticking my nose in their business.

Lucky for me, Aurora is of the same mind. "That's right! Don't judge so harshly, boys. You don't know her story or the circumstances of her life."

Not one of them comes back with a witty retort or different opinion. They do not even mind that their mother still calls them boys. They find her charming. It's obvious.

And she deserves the title. They are each man enough to know Aurora's opinion is not formed lightly. I think they respect her so much they listen. This is very encouraging. If ever Nobel and I have a child, they will have a smart Grandmother and a great role model. God. Did I just go there?

"But she did have a beautiful body," she adds much to the men's delight. They start talking at once. For this they have all kinds of things to say, including Sam and Teddy who never met the woman.

Parish and Scarlett bring up the rear with a rolling cooler and their dog Boo in tow. As soon as they're out of the car Maudie starts barking excitedly. I have never heard her strong bark. She can't sustain it, but the will is there. It's so touching. This is going to be the best party.

13
Nobel

I admit it's fun. This birthday business feels different than I thought it would. It's comfortable with Dove by my side. She fits in with all the personalities. Not just fits. She elevates conversations with a kind of positive, sunny influence. She calls people out on their bullshit, but in a nice way. All she does is ask the right questions. Interesting.

There's already enough of our dry humor and light cynicism to go around. She adds to the positive, right next to the parents. And they really like her. I can tell they all do. Not sure how she does it, but Aargon has talked more tonight than the last two years combined. I actually saw him laugh out loud, like he used to when his wife was alive. Maybe he just needs to be reminded what a woman can do for a man's mindset. I hope so.

The dining table is cleared, except for the shot glasses and bottle of tequila my father just brought in.

"Oh yeah! Let's do that," Van says, giving himself the first pour.

He passes the bottle around the table and every glass is filled.

"Everybody in?" He says it as if someone here is going to refuse. I know that's not going to happen.

"What about us?" Teddy says, already knowing the answer.

"Forget it," Aargon says.

Two dejected faces say a mouthful.

Dove speaks up. "This is going to be a drinking game. And we all know what it is except for Nobel."

"Uh-oh," I say and mean it.

"You're going to hate it," Van says, sure of himself.

"Stop it! He's going to be a good sport," my mother says.

This scares me more than anything. "Wait! What kind of game?"

Dove ignores me completely. So does the rest of them.

"Okay. Nobel needs to take his place in the living room, and then Gaston will blindfold him while the rest of us prepare."

"Blindfold? Should I hate this already?" I say without a hint of sarcasm.

"No! You should be excited," Scarlett adds. "Your woman put a lot of thought into this."

"Come on, everyone, let's raise our glasses to the birthday boy!" Dove calls and then downs the fiery liquid in one gulp.

Hell, why not? We all follow her lead.

"Smooth," Gaston says.

"Awwww!" My mother reacts strongly as the fire makes its way down her throat. "I like it," she adds, making us laugh.

"Gaston, will you take Nobel to his spot please? So we can prepare."

Prepare? This may be way out of my wheelhouse. No, it definitely is, I know it. Okay man just go with whatever she has planned. It's not going to kill you. Or if it does it will be over soon.

"Come on, son," my father says, rising from the chair.

I follow his lead, heading for my assigned seat.

"Gaston! Bring the tequila and your and Nobel's shot glasses," Aurora calls from the other room.

He grabs the bottle off the table, and I take the glasses.

"This is so fun!" Scarlett calls.

The sound of whispers and laughter follow me into the living room, fading as we get further away.

"Hey Dad, fill me in. What has she planned?" I whisper my request hoping we can form an alliance. I've been watching too many reality shows with Dove.

He looks at me as if I'm about to be committed. "That's not going to happen. Just sit here and enjoy it."

"Do I really have to participate?"

"Don't be a tight ass. You're going to like it."

I haven't been called that since he tried to get me to take his bookkeeper's pissy daughter out in high school. The stupid part of the story was that my father was the one who had previously told me about her shitty attitude. When I pointed out I could choose my own dates, he said 'Well get to it, son. You're not getting any younger. And quit being a tight ass.'

So I take his remark in the spirit it was intended. Fatherly guidance.

"Okay. Okay. I'm in."

There are new sounds now. That's when the red blindfold in his pocket gets tied around my eyes. I recognize the silky square Dove and I have used to tie her wrists in the bedroom. Ha! Think my girl is sending me a private joke. Love the way she thinks.

"And don't look out the bottom," he says, adjusting the folds over every possible sliver of light.

"I can't see a thing, Dad. Quit pushing on my eyes!"

"Okay. Sorry that's good I think."

I hear footsteps going away from the dining room and

kitchen and moving toward the guest rooms. But I knew that already. Whatever is in there requires multiple people to carry it, or maybe assemble? No, they wouldn't wait till now to do that.

What kind of noise was that? Sounded like bells. Or maybe a chime? It is directly followed by people shushing each other and laughing. It brings a smile to my face. Now there are a few people coming into the room. Something heavy is being rolled across the wood floors.

"Where do you want it?" Parish whispers.

"Dude, he can hear us! His ears aren't covered," Van says, making my father laugh.

"You guys, over here!" Dove says, directing traffic.

"Be careful!" my mother says to someone.

"Careful of what?" I say, getting more confused by the minute.

"It will all be revealed soon!" Scarlett adds in the voice of a prophet.

Another clue. "What's that? Sounds like a tambourine! Aargon is in the house!" I say, beginning to put the puzzle pieces together.

"Shut up! Just wait one more minute," Aargon says, walking from the hall into the room.

"Oh I must be close. Is it something musical? Are we playing Name That Tune? That's it. We used to play that when we were young."

"We're still young!" Van says, laying something metal on the coffee table. "At least I am."

More footsteps and voices.

"Are we all ready?" Dove says. "Yes. Okay, Nobel you may remove your blindfold."

As soon as I lower the scarf, I'm greeted with an onslaught of sound coming from The Lyon Family Birthday Band. The matching T-shirts declare the group's professional name. Everyone plays some kind of instrument, from Sam and Teddy's actual guitars to Aargon's old tambourine. My mother has a kazoo I've never seen. She hands my father one of his own, which he immediately begins to toot. Scarlett and Parish represent the drum section with a bongo between his legs and a child's drum hanging around her neck. Van is the pianist and that is probably because he took piano lessons longer than the rest of us. The portable keyboard works for his limited skills. Happy Birthday was his opus back in the day when anything more sophisticated was out of his reach. He played it fourteen thousand times back in the day. Dove holds a cowbell and she's ringing it at the right spots.

"More cowbell!" I holler.

I think they are still playing Happy Birthday but it's hard to tell because of the laughter and the fact they have to start over three times. Whatever it is, I love that they're doing it for me. The lump in my throat will have to stay there though, because I'm not about to get emotional over a happy birthday song.

Dove dances around the group, cowbell in hand. As she passes Aargon he follows her lead forming an impromptu conga line that winds around the room and passes in front of my chair. Only the two guitarists and Van stay in their places. Parish and Scarlett beat their drums in time. My mother and father add a kazoo dance linking arms. Van can't take being out of the loop any longer, and rises with the keyboard cradled in one arm, joining his fellow band members. Not sure he's hit a right note since he stood.

It comes to an abrupt end when the keyboard falls and crashes to the floor. The edge of the board breaks off and slides under the coffee table.

"Ta da!" he says as a flourish as the last notes fade in an uneven finish. The kazoos and guitars are the last to sound.

I applaud and stand for the performers. They are clapping for themselves too. And laughing.

"Bravo!" I call. Bravo!"

Everyone is talking at once.

"That was so much fun!" Scarlett says, giving Parish a peck.

Pointing at Sam and Teddy I give them their due with a thumbs up.

"Very nice! Whose idea was this?"

"Three guesses," Sam says. "And the first two don't count."

I look to Dove, and she smiles with my words. "It was you, right?'

"Of course it was her! We wouldn't have had the balls," Van says, getting on his hands and knees to retrieve the piece of plastic.

I walk to her and take her in my arms. "Thank you, babe. It was awesome."

"We aren't done yet. That was just the start of tonight's festivities."

She untangles from my hold and speaks to the group. "It's karaoke time! Grab your shot glasses!"

"What? Oh no. Not me. But you guys do it for sure," I say, knowing my opinion is going to be rejected.

The room talks back.

My mother gives me "the look" and points her finger.

"Don't be silly! Of course you're going to participate. Your girl went to a lot of trouble."

"If Parish can do it so can you," says Scarlett.

"Just do it. You are never gonna get out of it," Van adds.

Dove ignores the whole thing. She knows perfectly well I will capitulate.

"All right, all right. Maybe one song. And someone has to sing with me. I don't know the words of songs! Shit!"

"I call bullshit," Argon says, smiling like the Cheshire Cat. "You know one for sure."

Van starts laughing. Oh crap. I know exactly what he's thinking. "Louie Louie's" infamous dirty lyrics were enjoyed by The Lyon brothers, ad nauseam.

"I have to be drunker than I am to sing that one. It's not for mixed company."

"Listen, take your seats and this can be informal. The lyrics are on the screen if you can't recall them. But this is a night for fun, so there are no wrong lyrics or bad voices," Dove instructs. "We also have your songs on a playlist and you can sing along with the original artist if you feel better doing that."

"That's right. You can do a group singalong or go it on your own. Who wants to go first?" My father is into this whole thing, it's obvious he's raring to go.

"Gaston, why don't you start? Oh! And every time a new performer comes to the stage, we have to take a shot!"

That gets everyone's attention. Van's all for it, but looks like he and Dove are alone in their opinion.

"We will be on the floor by the fourth singer! Let's do every other song. Or third one," the voice of reason says.

"You're right, Aurora. Okay, every third song. Because once this gets going, we could be singing for hours."

My woman has faith in her ideas. I reach for one of the tequila bottles on the coffee table and pour myself a shot of liquid courage. Dad lifts his and Mom's glasses and I fill theirs too.

"To my family. Glad I landed in your world."

There are toasts all around, and once again the two teenagers are bummed with their Cokes. My father rises and makes his way to the karaoke machine and microphone.

"Testing, one, two, three."

"What are you going to sing, Grandpa?" Teddy asks.

"Teddy, my first selection..."

He's interrupted by the rooms' reactions. Laughter mostly.

"First? How many are you going to delight us with tonight?" Aargon says.

"As many as you request, son. I don't really see the night ending early."

The tequila is downed, and he clears his throat.

"As I was saying, my first choice is a song that has meant so much to me over the years. I think we should start with a love song. You will know it too and I encourage anyone who does to sing along. Don't be embarrassed that I happen to be a better singer than any of you."

He eyes Dove and rethinks his last comment. "With one exception that is."

"Thank you, Gaston."

"Hey, what about us?" Sam says loudly.

"Yeah! We both sing in our band."

"Okay, okay. I'm the best singer with the exception of Dove, Sam, and Teddy. But that's it."

"Mom's got a pretty voice," Scarlett adds.

"Jesus, people! I guess you are all better than me. Just shut the hell up and enjoy the performance!"

We are laughing so hard and the singing hasn't started yet. A nod from my dad signals Dove to play the chosen song. "Brick House" begins to the screams of laughter from the audience.

"Love song?" Sam says.

"Most definitely. I hear ya, Dad!" Van calls between the beat.

Watching my parents groove to their generation's music is something great. I don't know how they did it, but my father still sees my mother as that young woman he wanted to sleep with. And she sees him as the sexy bohemian artist with a cut body. For them, things have not changed.

We all know the words to the Commodores' classic seventies song. Parish and Scarlett are dancing with their drums and Teddy and Sam accompany on guitar. Whether the woman in the song is mighty mighty or letting it all hang out, everyone here can identify with the image. Even the kids. I think back to when I was sixteen and wanting to lose my virginity.

As the tune ends, my mother rises and wraps her arms around the singer, who is happy to oblige.

"That was great, Gaston! Let's give our first performer a big round of applause!" Dove says clapping.

"I'll go next. I can't be any worse than the last guy," Van says.

"That's gratitude for you. I taught you how to piss remember."

Sam and Teddy find that very funny.

"And I thank you for that, Dad. I might not have figured it out on my own."

"Smart ass."

Picking up the mic, Van announces his selection in soft reverent tones. "The boys and I are going to be singing one of *our* favorites and an ode to women everywhere, "Baby Got Back" by Sir Mix A Lot. Also known as I Like Big Butts. We have spent two weeks memorizing this, so we deserve best of the night. Just sayin'."

The boys take their places on either side of their uncle and leave their guitars behind. Out of a bag next to the karaoke machine come two cheap blonde wigs which they quickly don. They are the backup singers I take it. Dove finds the tune on the playlist and hits play. The sound of two girls talking about big asses tells me this is the extended explicit version. Sam and Teddy play the girls perfectly, mouthing the dialogue and overacting their parts. That's what makes it funny.

Itty bitty waists and round things in your face bring smiles and laughter and more than one person sings along. Specifically Scarlett, Parish, and my father. Why am I surprised he knows the words? Of course he does. Aargon stays silent, but he's loving it too. When Van compares himself to a turbo Vette, my mother's mouth drops in fake insult. She's digging it just like the rest of us.

When the song ends, the guys get a huge round of applause.

"I told you," Van says, proud of the performance. He bows and the boys follow suit.

"This is the third song coming up. Tequila time. Gaston, will you do the honors?" Dove says.

"Yes, of course. I pour a proper shot."

"Which is actually two at once," my mother says. "I guess I'll go," she says standing.

Taking her place in front of the family she takes the microphone.

"My selection is "Dream a Little Dream of Me" made famous by Mama Cass. This is the song I sang to all my children when I tucked them in. I hope it brings back good memories. Tonight, it is dedicated to Mr. Invisible. Happy birthday, son. I love you dearly."

Oh shit. A note hasn't been sung yet, and there's a lump in my throat. Lucky for me, there are tears in Aragon's eyes and Scarlett's so I won't be the only crybaby. Van's head is hung, but I expect he feels the same way. Dove is biting her lip. Only the boys are clueless what this means to us.

With a nod to Dove, the opening notes fill the room. My heart is full too. Full of the sweetness of my mother and all the ways she gave love to her children. The voice is soft and pure, just as I remember. When she sings say nitey nite and kiss me, I'm transported back to the old bedroom, where the three of us boys slept in bunk beds. I remember hearing the same goodnight song through the wall as she would sing to Kristen and Scarlett.

Whatever my dreams may be, she asks that I dream a little dream of her. Looking across the room I see Parish holding back his emotions. The loss he suffered years back surfaces every so often in tears that are impossible to stop. That's what Scarlett told me once when we were talking about his young son's fatal shooting. She takes his hand, and he holds on tight. I see the white knuckles from here.

Oh hell. That does it. A fat tear streams down my cheek and my brothers look like they're feeling it too. Now Dad lets go. And when he does, Mom gets choked up too.

I've learned you never know what is going to trigger memories of Kristen. The whistle at the end of the song was always our young selves' favorite part, because mom's the best whistler in the family. But tonight, it is broken up by a tight throat.

"That's it! Oh my God. Didn't mean to make us upset. I'm sorry. It's just that the memory is one of my favorites. I miss those early days."

I get up and go to her, taking her in my arms and whispering in her ear, "I love you, Mom. Thank you for everything."

She whispers back, "Love you too, son. More than you could ever know."

"This calls for another shot," Aargon says, grabbing the bottle.

"Give me some of that," Parish adds.

No one argues the point. Rules or not. Scarlett stands.

"Okay. I hereby proclaim a change of mood. Our turn. It's going to be a trio. Parish and Aargon are not interested in performing. But I am! So, eyes on me, and hopefully they make it through an entire song without having heart attacks."

"Oh God. Let's get it over with," Aargon says, joining my sister and soon to be brother-in-law. He downs the tequila and wipes away the last of the tears.

"Hit it," Parish says.

"Wait! The hats!"

She digs in the bag and comes out with three baseball caps. Hers says Star and theirs each say Stick In The Mud #1 and Stick In The Mud #2. As the familiar song begins, Scarlett is dancing around the room to the familiar instrumental, using arms and hips to make her point. Thing 1 and 2 have borrowed the parents' kazoos, and they stand blowing the general tune and pouring fresh shots. But the laughter from the family, and their general haze of alcohol, amuses them so much they begin to get into the spirit.

As their big moment arrives, they shout, "Tequila!" And so does everyone else.

Scarlett's dancing recital continues, but it's the two drunks that have the spotlight. When Aargon attempts a move that requires more talent than simply standing, he gets off balance. Thing 2 comes to his aid with an outstretched arm. Parish shouts, "Tequila!" But it isn't the right time. He's ahead of the lyric and that is funnier to them and us than if he had been on target.

"You assholes!" Scarlett yells across the room. But she's laughing. "You're ruining my performance!"

"I have to sit down," Aargon suddenly says.

"Help him, Parish."

"Me help him? Okay."

The song continues to play and builds to its final notes, but all eyes are on my brother as he flops down in the club chair. And at the right moment he looks up through bloodshot eyes and says, "Tequila!"

"Oh Lord," my mother says.

The drunk looks up for a moment. "I'm good. Continue."

Dove gets ahold of the microphone and takes charge.

"That leaves Nobel and me."

My expression sends her a message. Can you do this without me? She retrieves a barstool sitting behind the karaoke machine and pats the seat. Van moves another right next to it.

"Come on, get up here. I have something picked out for us and it won't hurt too much, all you have to do is sit and look at me adoringly. Come on, baby."

Aargon perks up.

"Ohhhhh. You calling him baby? I like it, Dove. He is a big baby."

The insult only worked when we were between the ages of five and eight. He used to call me that and the words would make me totally pissed off crazy. In our young world, there was no greater put down than being accused of being babyish. The moniker lost its sting about thirty-five years ago. But that's what makes this funny. He knows it too and chuckles in his stupor.

I rise and head for the stage. I'm very happy about this new direction. No singing, and I can look at her adoringly all day. As I sit, she gives me a quick kiss.

"This is for my birthday boy."

She nods to Teddy and he presses a button on the karaoke machine. The opening notes of Rihanna's "Stay" begin. I told her I thought of us whenever I heard this song. The room quiets to listen and to watch as she gives of herself to the person and everyone is charmed. Tonight the gift comes to me, even though in my heart I know it's meant for the world. But God knows I want her to stay.

14

Dove

Adjusting the skirt of the dress, I catch my barefoot image in the dressing room mirror.

"What about this one?"

Deborah is a reliable judge of what looks good on me or not. She's rarely critical but always truthful. That talent has been honed over the years. I rely on her take more than my own. Almost all of my stage clothes she has picked.

"I still like the first one. It shows off your legs. Besides, the color is gorgeous."

Looking in Macy's mirror I get her point. This is beautiful but a little generic.

"Let me try it on one more time," I say, peeling off the rejected frock.

"Are we sure showing off my legs is a good idea at a wedding? I don't want to look like I'm going to the club."

I step into the royal blue, discounted, affordable designer dress.

"It's a good idea. Play to your strength."

"This one is seventy-nine. It's pretty pathetic. I can barely afford that much. But it's good, right?"

Before Deborah answers a familiar ping sounds. I got a text.

"Let me see who this is."

Retrieving the phone sitting atop my purse, I stare at the name. Arthur James? Arthur James!!

"Oh my God!" I holler.

Deborah, who had been looking down at her own phone, jumps with my scream. "Fuck! You scared the shit out of me!"

I turn the screen to her.

"Oh my God! What did he say? Read it!"

With shaking hands, I bring up the text. I can't help but remember the unfortunate circumstances of our last phone conversation two years ago. Hope things have changed.

Arthur: Afternoon, Dove. I was given a cut of your song "Mined" recorded at Cosgrove Studios in May. I'd like to speak with you. Are you and the band available for a Zoom call tomorrow at one?

"He wants to have a Zoom call tomorrow. With the band."

That's all I can get out before tears blur the screen and interrupt the words.

"Answer him!! Oh, Dove."

"Don't you want to? Shouldn't it come from our manager?"

"Not this time. I think you should make the personal connection. Let's see what he has to say."

Her arms surround me with the compassion and shared joy only a best friend can offer. And the excitement a manager does. She is the only person outside the band that understands what this could mean to us. Could being the operative word. I untangle and try to compose the right response.

"Okay, help me. I don't want to sound anxious or blasé. What should I say?"

"Say yes."

One text, four excited calls from the car, and for Deborah and me a rehashing of our shared history with Arthur. It fills the half hour it takes to get back home. Everyone is already there waiting as we pull in the driveway. I'm out of the car, running toward the men and screaming my happiness. Four faces tell the same story. ZZ's half-smile lifting the corners of his mouth equals the same sense of excitement. That is his unbridled joy. Jimmy wears the biggest smile. I jump in Tony's outstretched arms and he twirls me around.

"Is this really happening?" he says. "You better not be bullshitting."

"Do you think I'd be that cruel? Come on."

"Do you think he's gonna offer us a contract?" Oscar asks, following me to the door.

"I don't know. Maybe. We got close before."

We enter the house and Deborah goes for the refrigerator. "I'm going to get us some beer."

The purse gets thrown to the floor under the window and I join Tony and Jimmy on the couch. I look Jimmy in the eyes and ask the question I know he'll have a thoughtful opinion about.

"I mean we don't want to get ahead of ourselves, but this looks pretty good, right? Please say yes."

A big sigh precedes the answer. "Yes. And the best part is the fact he's interested in an original song."

I start to react before I weigh my actions, but at the last moment resist kissing him on the cheek. It's just that I feel such love for all the guys. It would be so natural under normal circumstances. But our relationship hasn't found its new normal yet. Even after all this time. So instead of a kiss he gets my most enthusiastic high five.

"Let's talk about our options should we get an offer," Deborah says, passing a beer to Tony.

She tosses one to ZZ. We all have our preferences and for Jimmy and me beer doesn't do it.

"Want a Coke?" Deborah says.

"I'm good."

She grabs a seat in the club chair. "I don't think we can continue to use Brian as our attorney. He just doesn't have the experience we are going to need. I'll start looking. We're not going to have anything by tomorrow. And Arthur knows it. He knows it all remember. We're not going to outfox the fox."

"You're right. Better we approach this authentically," I add. "No bullshit. Let's expect to be respected as artists and he'll know we will hire representation if we have an offer."

"That's all good. But this isn't puppies and rainbows. This is the business of music. Better that we present ourselves in a professional manner. That's what will be respected," she says.

"We shouldn't make anyone think we undervalue our worth," ZZ adds in a calm tone.

That begins a long meaningful conversation about goals and plans. Dreams. We are clearly out of our depth. But we are dreamers, all. How ours may be about to come true is mind-blowing. Are we getting a second chance? Is everyone prepared to grasp the golden ring? We each are prepared to commit. In the biography of our lives this will go down as one of the best days. It's all hope. I've always embraced uncertainty and trusted the wait.

. . .

"That's great, Dove."

Nobel says it with a smile. I can tell he wants to be supportive, but what's with the lack of enthusiasm? Am I misreading his face in the ambient light of the restaurant? Maybe I haven't explained the weight of what happened today. I try again.

"No, it's really a big deal. Let me give you some background. A few years back this producer that called today, Arthur, saw one of our shows in Nashville. We had gone there for a week's run at this tiny but kind of famous music venue. Anyway, apparently he liked what he saw and contacted us."

All this time Nobel remains silent, just taking in the words. But behind his eyes I see a seed of unhappiness. What? No. I have to be wrong about that.

"So long story short, we were offered an opening act contract for a popular mid-level band that was going on a tour of the south in the summer. We were about to move to Nashville as a home base. It was a break we'd only dreamed of."

"What happened? I don't remember you saying you ever were on tour."

I dab the napkin to my lips and set it on the table. "We never were. Before the contracts were negotiated and signed, my grandfather got sick. There was no one else to care for him. It came down to me and nothing was going to stop me from being his champion. I had to turn the offer down."

His eyes soften now and the real Nobel returns. "What did your band members say?"

"It was a big blow, but what could they say? These are my actual friends. In the end they were required to understand because the offer wasn't for four of us. It was all or none. They could not do it without me. But believe me we understand we're greater than the sum of our parts and only work together anyway."

"Couldn't you hire someone to care for your grandfather?"

I lock eyes with him across the table. "Would you leave your dog to a stranger as she was dying?"

A shake of his head answers my pointed question.

"I commend you. I'm sure your grandfather was grateful."

"He never knew."

"What?"

"I wasn't about to tell him how inconvenient his dying was for me. This is a man who sacrificed so I would have a family and know love. He and my grandmother fed my dream and acted like I was the most talented singer that ever lived. They wanted my success. If he knew, it would have been devastating. I think he deserved to be protected from the truth."

"Wow."

"I told him the offer fell through."

"I understand. Why didn't you get ahold of Arthur after your grandfather passed away?"

"Oh, we tried. There wasn't the same interest. We had missed our spot. Passing up an offer to tour was a sign to them we were not all in, not dedicated to our craft. He said as much the one time he did respond to our attempts to talk."

He signals the server for our check, then turns back to me. I still see he is disturbed.

"What's this?" I say, pointing a finger to his expression.

It's surprising he doesn't pretend ignorance. Instead, he doubles down.

"What does this mean for us? Are you going to go on tour for a year? Will we be apart?"

"I understand your concern Nobel, but the answer is maybe, if we are extremely lucky. Yes, it could happen. Or maybe it's all about releasing our latest song and recording more. That would require time spent in Nashville. But we can figure out a way through this that satisfies us both. There's planes and trains and automobiles. There are phones. You have a job that is flexible. That alone works to our advantage."

"What do you mean?"

"I mean you can come along. Be with me. If Nashville is the place I need to be, then we will learn to love it. What would be stopping you?" I say it with the enthusiasm felt. It seems so obvious to me. Why not to him?

"Uh, my life, my job, the home, Maudie, the family. Shall I go on? I mean it's not that simple, Dove."

"As far as I can see, it's only Maudie that needs to come first. You said not two weeks ago you could work from anywhere in the United States. Your family? They would be happy for your adventure. Your house? It doesn't need you. You have a security system, and you can come back and check in whenever you'd feel the urge. And your life? Whether we are together for one year or a hundred, it should be thought of as *our* life."

"Well, yes. That's true."

"Then you should know that sometimes in *our* life, my goals and dreams will take first place. Being together will require us both to make sacrifices at different times. I've already proved how devoted I can be to those I love. I have put myself second. I think we need to demonstrate we support the aim of the other. Are you willing to do that, especially when it's so simple for you to do?"

"Of course, I support you."

He knows I'm right, but it's just too far out of his comfort zone to say more. Did he think I was going to lose the lifelong dream? No, my love. I can love you *and* catch a star. Come along with me. I want it more than you could possibly know. And by that I mean the dream and you.

That dark expression makes me think the electric chair is waiting for his occupancy just outside the restaurant. Dead man walking. He notices my eyes taking it all in, and switches channels.

"Let's go home and salvage the day," he says smiling.

I reach for his hand. "Good thinking, baby."

All the way back we're playing grab ass with each other. It seemed like it took an hour to get from the restaurant to his driveway. I'd say both of us have come to the conclusion distraction is the best way forward. At least for a night. I rub the back of his neck, he runs a hand over my leg. There's little conversation but it's not uncomfortable. The previous discussion has to settle first. For us both. He is adjusting to the idea of a different kind of life and I'm juggling with knowing how difficult it will be for him. Sex and affection are great tools to remind us of our bond.

It isn't easy for either to realize we may be faced with a life changing decision so soon in our relationship. But I can't ignore what I know. Nobel and I are meant. To be together, to love, and to find a way through whatever obstacles present themselves. This is life. If we want to be together, it's within our power to make it happen.

"I can't wait to get in bed and just let the day go," he says, shutting off the motor.

"Me too. I don't want to think of anything other than the healing touch of your hands on my body. Let's go."

He's looking at the side window of the front door and his brows come together.

"What?"

"Maudie isn't greeting us. It's kind of strange."

The pit of my stomach tightens.

"She's probably sleeping. Her hearing is getting worse."

"True. That's it. Okay, let's go in."

Exiting the car, we climb the steps and I sense a fear in

him. And me if I'm being honest. Oh please Maudie. Be there. Be there. Nobel wastes no time getting the key in, and just as he does, I see Maudie through the window. Her eyes are open as she lays on the floor by the window.

"There she is!" I say with the relief that floods my body.

His attention is pulled to the window.

"Hi my girl! Fuck you scared the shit out of me," he says as the door swings open.

But as we enter and he gets on his knees to embrace the dog, I see the change in her. Something is different. Off. As Nobel's hands pet her coat and he offers loving words, she tries getting up. A sharp whine sounds and then leaves as quickly as it came.

"Her arthritis must be especially bad. Poor baby. I'm going to warm your pad. Let me get that going. Dove, will you get a biscuit for her?"

He wants to believe the pain comes from the arthritis and ignore the fact she is also suffering from the pain of the cancer. I think in his mind it sounds like a solvable problem. Something to wrap his head around when the truth can't be faced. He's pretending because it is so painful to know there isn't a thing he can do to fix the problem. He cannot save the dog he loves with all his heart.

"Yeah. Is it time for the pain med yet? Want me to bring it?"

I throw my bag to a chair and head for the kitchen island.

"She still has an hour to go but fuck it. Yeah, bring it please. And a piece of cheese so I can get it down her throat."

I return with the three items. The pill gets hidden in the cheese, but when he tries to get Maudie to swallow, it's a no go. She will not take it. Nobel tries repeatedly and with each attempt he is getting more disturbed.

"Come on, baby. This will make you feel better. Please. Take it. Umm, cheese."

I see a tear course down his cheek, which he quickly wipes away. Maudie rests her head on the cool floor and closes her eyes. I'm not sure she has the strength to walk to her bed. I try to come up with some positive spin on the disturbing scene.

"The pain seems to have stopped. Maybe she just wants to sleep right there."

He grabs ahold of my delusion and joins me.

"You're right. Let me get the bed and bring it to her here in case she wants to use it."

Rising, he grabs the warm, cushy oval and lays it right against her, so she feels it. The dog stays where she is. So, he gently lifts her and transfers her thin body to the warmth of the bed.

When I look in his eyes, they are full of tears. Oh damn! Now mine. I let mine go, in hopes he will use them as permission to cry. It takes a moment, but he does. We hold each other closely and I can feel the sadness envelop his body as he cries. But I don't look at Nobel's face. I don't want to do anything that will make him hold back the emotions that are begging to be let out. I say nothing until he does.

"God, what a baby I am."

I take his face in my hands. He looks at me and I see despair. I feel the helplessness.

"No, you're not a baby. You are a man who knows how to love another being. Dog or person. This is the appropriate response, Nobel. You're losing someone you adore."

Another fat tear streams down his face and he hangs his head.

"I think she's okay right now. She isn't showing any more pain and she's resting. What say we spend the night down here with her?"

Now he locks watery eyes with me.

"Yes. I want to be close."

"Me too. We can light a fire and put on some classical music like you said she likes. Does that sound right?"

"Yeah. Good idea."

"Okay I'm going to get our pillows and change into my sweats. I'll bring yours down."

He kisses the top of my head and it's so meaningful in its tenderness.

"Thank you."

I untangle my arms from his, grab my purse and head for the stairs. On the way up I dig for the cell and check the messages. Deborah, Jimmy. I stop there. Jimmy never calls unless it is important, necessary or someone died. Not since our messy chapter. I listen to his voicemail.

"Hey. Arthur sent a group text. Did you get it? Where are you? Call me."

There's a bit of impatience in his tone. That's weird. But as I reach the top of the stairs, I see why. I missed the bell, alerting me to all these texts. Oh, it was at seven. We were in the restaurant. I had turned the phone off to give my full attention to Nobel. It was the right move on one level, but I can't do that after tonight. This is too important.

Arthur: Need to add another Zoom call. We will talk tomorrow as planned, but there's another interested party. Archangel is going to be in the studio when you're here. They want to sit in on the session. I said yes. He will be calling you at 1:30. It's hard to pin this guy down, so make sure you've locked in the time. Confirm please. Arthur.

Archangel? The country band that is making waves with their first album likes our music? A flush of energy courses through my body. But it's followed by the realization Saturday is

Scarlett and Parish's wedding day. Ohhh shit. Shit. Fucking shit!! There's no choice. If I take the call at that time, we should be finished by three at the latest. The ceremony is at three so I could probably make it to the reception before the first dance. Nobel will just have to understand. Oh yeah, that's going to happen.

I catch myself. Wait. This is how it is going to be from now on. Grabbing the brass ring requires you to be on the carousel. I have an invitation that won't be extended indefinitely. It's now. We will have to roll with whatever comes our way, knowing that if we are solid things will work. *Stop!*

Tonight is not the time for relaying my news or debating the details of our relationship. No way. This is Maudie's time. And Nobel's.

"Dove! Bring my grey blanket that's on the chair!"

The voice snaps me out of my own story. The million pieces that are floating in my head dissolve. Back to earth.

15

Nobel and Maudie

I take the blanket from Dove and tuck it around Maudie. There is an elevated state that reveals itself in a dog's face. A kind of holiness. It redefines usual descriptions of what constitutes beauty. It is more than that. We are lifted higher with their loving gaze.

She's so still. Except for the breathing. It has become more labored. Puffs of air come out of her snout and there is a shallowness to them. When asked, the vet told me what to look for if death was close. I thought I was asking prematurely, but I was not. Things have progressed. It has come too quickly. Thought we might have another six months at least. Fuck. No matter how I spin what is happening, I return to the same conclusion and undeniable truth. She's dying. My sweet girl is dying.

It's strange what you wish for when time runs short. It's not anything grand. It's not a run in the field or a splash in the river. It isn't a thrown ball I want to see her retrieve. It's only a little time, the vanishing commodity. I want another day, even just half of one. I'd sit with her and let her have my sweater as a blanket to rest a head on. She likes the smell of her human.

I would look in her eyes and try to describe the color and shape. Then I'd write it down so not to forget important details. Scratching those big ears, I'd go one minute longer than I ever had before. Maudie never tired of that. It would be me who would quit every time. I would say I love you in dog speak and listen to every conversation she offers with her tail and body language.

It has become clear something beautiful in my life is about to become a memory. It doesn't matter that it is in the form of canine as opposed to human. Real love cannot distinguish the difference. I will go to my own grave believing it is true.

If these are the final hours, my prayers beg for a gentle journey. The gifts she brought to my life deserve reward in her dark hour. Could she just fall asleep and when her eyes open be in Paradise? What can I do to help make that happen?

"Want me to get us some tea? Or maybe you want a whiskey?"

"No babe. Just bring me a water, okay?"

Dove moves to the kitchen and I resume petting my girl. I want to hold her paw. Very carefully, I pick it up and cup it in my palm. I hope she knows I am with her.

Little soft sounds rise in Maudie and her eyelids flutter. I don't think it's pain. It is more like a response to some scene playing out in her mind. Like when she dreams. Is she running with Boo through the trees? Is she watching the sunset from the porch? Does she see me there with her? Or are the animals we loved before gathered in excitement on the Rainbow Bridge awaiting her arrival and she can see them? An almost imperceptible wag of her tail is the last movement she makes before her heart quiets. I begin to sob.

16
Nobel

The priest directs his pointed comment at Van who happens to be fucking around with Scarlett's friend Aby, the bridesmaid. They have decided to dance up the aisle to the violin and harp music.

"This isn't rocket science, just move forward at an even pace people." He claps his meaty hands in rhythm.

Reverend Ralph has a disgusted look on his face. He does not suffer fools lightly. It may not be priestly, but it is funny. I imagine some future sheet cake with the man's words spelled out in red letters. My brother, and the woman he currently is targeting for a wedding day hookup, stop the bullshit and get on board. I think Scarlett's evil eye made its point.

We won't be punished for any church infraction. My brothers and I have done much worse in here and gotten away with every one. Like putting a condom on St. Peter's statue. It was a job for The Invisible Man, and totally worth the risk of being discovered. I don't think I ever made my brothers laugh so much. I gained their respect with that one. They figured I was just as twisted as they were. Invisible or not. The story wasn't admitted until I was in my twenties. By then no one gave a shit.

My parents are probably reliving their own wedding, when they were married by the Reverend. They were all young then. Younger than we are now by twenty years. It's hard to picture them as innocents. Father Ralph had just been transferred from another parish and according to the descriptions just as cynical as he is today. Baptisms, confirmations, and every other sacrament we were part of has involved him in some way.

It's kind of funny only one Lyon kid has stayed in the Church. And it isn't the bride. Ralph doesn't need to know what Scarlett thinks about his church. She respects him and family tradition, and that is enough for her. Ironically, it is Van who still attends Mass and considers himself Catholic. Maybe he still likes to cruise women in the congregation like he did at sixteen.

I make eye contact with Dove who sits patiently in a long almost empty pew. She winks. Two rows ahead sit my parents, behind them Teddy and Sam. Parish's sister and his family are across the aisle. So far the rehearsal has gone pretty smoothly. It's a happy group.

My sister and her man deserve the joy. That's how I feel about their traumatic story. I know being a good person doesn't guarantee smooth sailing in life. But if there is karma or justice of any kind in this world, she and Parish would reap the reward. Scarlett's sacrifice for Sam alone is worthy of all things good. She put her whole life on hold to make sure he survived his mother and father's deaths.

The fact Scarlett was processing it at the same time speaks to her strength. It was up to her and she came through with flying colors. Not an easy task for a childless, young woman. She left us to be with Sam and navigate his initial grief after the car accident. Just as Kristen would have wanted. It was a beautiful thing. Kind of holy in a way.

Life is odd, though. In doing that she ended up meeting Parish. Think she saved him too. Because according to him he was living a cliche'. A writer turning into an alcoholic. She is our family's Joan of Arc and has earned our everlasting respect.

The groom must be feeling emotional as the wedding approaches. The death of his own child is something that is ever present, according to my sister. Just as our loss is. It follows you, whether you are living one of your best moments or worst. It stands silently, always within reach. Think all of us are coming to grips with that.

But I can't see any of it now. The bride and groom look like an enchanted spell has been placed on them. They are happy as fuck. I like that. Hope over despair. In fact, I have never seen Scarlett so over the moon. He does that to her. Like me and Dove. She does it for me, even though I'm not too happy right at this particular moment. Think I'm hiding it pretty successfully.

After Maudie's death, she waited a couple of days to lay the hammer down. She's going to miss the wedding. Every time I think of it I get pissed off. I know there's hardly a person here who would agree with me. In fact, I would bet they'd think I was being a selfish dick. But, that makes no difference. I am mad at the Universe if nothing else. There's no order to a life that can take a left turn so randomly. Why do some of us thrive on that? When you can plan for things and make room for small pivots in life it runs so much smoother. There are enough surprises to survive even then.

For Dove, even this rehearsal is going to be cut short. It's Montana World and we all just live in it. That sounded petty, even in my own mind. I don't give a damn. It's how I feel.

Couldn't they have scheduled their band meeting earlier in the day? I mean it's just to go over things that are etched in their minds. Now Dove is all excited about this Archangel guy. What exactly does he want? Dove was weird when I asked her the question. Maybe the music producer wants a second opinion on the band's music. Does it work like that? This is just the talking phase, as far as I know. It's only the beginning of the conversations. God, I sound like an old grumpy man who is pissed the kids are having too much fun. I imagine my eighty-five-year-old self shouting, 'Get off my lawn!'.

Taking the arm of my aisle mate, Meagan, I nod, and we begin the march. Aargon begged to be paired with cousin Jeri, because it is obvious my bridesmaid has her eye on him. Poor girl doesn't know he would rather shit in his hat than be pursued by a random woman for whom he has no interest. Too bad, because she seems nice and Aargon needs to have some real fun.

Following Reverend Ralph's frustrated instructions, we move in proper time toward the altar. When we arrive at Parish and Scarlett, we split, and she goes to the left while I join the groomsmen. Van, Aargon, and I stand next to the best man, Parish's brother.

When I look Dove's way, she makes a heart and points to me. Then she ups the ante. With exaggerated silent annunciation she says, "fuck me!". God, I love the irreverence in her. She would have been my partner in crime in school. Had she been born then. Shit. When we were in grade school, Dove wasn't even a twinkle in her father's eye.

My father catches me smiling like a goon. But when he sees where I'm looking he figures it out and smiles himself. My mother is looking at her children like she always has when we are together. With parental pride. It's really amazing how she kicks out all the shit we have put her through as kids and teenagers and focuses on what she wants to see. Wonder if I will ever know that feeling?

What are the chances of having children when my woman is the lead in a rock band? I can't picture a pregnant headliner. It doesn't elude me that I'm only concerned about my nonexistent family whenever it suits the argument. It sucks being self-aware.

I vaguely hear the priest's instructions to the bride and groom, because Dove has my attention. She looks at her watch. Catching my eye she smiles. There is a conversation happening between us made without words. I'm saying, can't I have your attention for the short time you are going to be here? She answers, don't get your boxer briefs in a twist.

"And then I tell you to kiss the bride."

Parish takes the opportunity to plant one on Scarlett. There's applause from the audience and even Reverend Ralph gets in the spirit by cracking a smile.

"That's it, folks. You let the bride and groom take the lead back down the aisle. You know the rest," he says, already heading for the sacristy. "See you tomorrow."

No one is surprised. There's alcohol waiting.

We scatter like ants and I head for Dove.

"You look very holy up there. I almost didn't recognize you with the halo," she says, standing.

"If you're a good girl I'll hear your confession later."

"I have no sins to confess," she teases. "Maybe I should hear yours."

"If you stay for the dinner, I'll tell you everything. All the dirty details of my impure thoughts."

I kiss her right in front of God and the saints watching from the sidelines of the room.

"Tempting. But I need to go. We're meeting at my place."

There's no use arguing the point. I know when to fold 'em.

"Okay. Drive safe. I should be home by nine. Nobody wants this to be a late night."

"Bye, baby. Have fun. I'll call you!"

And the girl is gone, leaving me stewing in a broth of unrighteous indignation. I know. But I can't stop myself.

The ride to the restaurant is at least distracting. Enlisting the company of Teddy and Sam was easy enough. Few sixteen-year-olds want to ride with their parents. I banked on that, remembering how it was back in the day.

Pulling into the parking lot brings back good memories. It's Scarlett's favorite from her childhood. All of us kids loved it. The Mountain Top looks a little timeworn now. Not just the Alpine façade, but the unchanged sign from nineteen ninety something. It seemed cool then, with a cartoon mountain climber about to slip off the edge. But we were looking through kids' eyes. Now it's only nostalgic.

"How come Dove isn't coming?" Sam asks.

I'm still getting used to his deep voice. It finally settled.

"She has a meeting with the band. Are you two bringing dates tomorrow?"

Laughter proceeds the answer. It's Teddy who spills the plan.

"No! We're taking Uncle Van's advice."

"Well, that's your first mistake," I say, unbuckling the seatbelt. "What pearls of wisdom did he tell you?"

As we exit the car, I see the look on their faces. Trouble.

Sam runs a hand through his thick hair and lays it out for me. "He said we should avoid bringing women to any wedding we go to from now on."

I know what is coming, but I want to hear it from them.

"Why is that?"

"Because a guy never knows who he's going to run into. We might meet some hot bridesmaids."

"The bridesmaids are all over twenty-five. Don't think you're going to have much luck there, guys."

I open the door and as Sam passes in front of me one eyebrow raises just like his mother's used to.

"The blonde was looking. Maybe she wants some of this," he says.

Their laughter and mine lifts my mood. Shit. The new generation of Lyons has already joined the game and I hardly noticed till now.

"Over here!" my father calls from the private room to the left.

The party has already started, with the bride and groom in animated conversations with their guests. Parish's brother and sister are footing the bill but despite that, their faces are as happy as our family's. I can tell from the way they interact the siblings share a close relationship.

It is kind of cool how people feel a different sort of joy at weddings. It's not like it's a new concept. We attend weddings all our lives and half of them end in divorce. Despite the fact, we act like we are just being introduced to real love. Everyone shares a collective hope. Maybe that is what has kept our species going. Denial. The feeling lives in this room right now. And this time, I believe it will last.

"Sit here!" my mother says, patting the empty seat next to her. Sam and Teddy claim the seats at the end of the rectangle table, and I slide in to mine.

"Want a cocktail?"

"No thanks. I'm saving the drinking for tomorrow. This water is good."

A server stands next to the bride and groom, waiting for instructions.

"We're ordering for the table. Schnitzel and sausages, there will be something for everyone. Is that okay?" Scarlett asks the guests.

There's agreement all around and the conversations resume. My mother's hand lands on mine and her eyebrows knit together.

"What's happening? Why the face?"

Denial won't work. She figured me out long ago. It's a given we all can trust her and more than that, respect her take on things.

"It's this Nashville thing I told you about. Well, that's not even happening yet. It's just a maybe."

"What about it?"

"I don't think distance is a good thing for a relationship."

By the questioning look on her face, I need to be clear.

"I mean, she has a great gig here."

"Do you mean you have a great gig here?"

As the words spilled from my mouth, I heard the weakness of my argument. My mother doesn't say another word. She just looks with that all knowing expression waiting for me to come to the right conclusion on my own. It worked when I was ten. But it's not that way this time. Not that easy. I wait her out.

"Listen to yourself, Nobel. First of all, who are you to choose how she navigates her career? You're in love with the girl?"

"Yes."

"Do you realize she's an artist?"

"Well, yeah."

"Then treat her like one. It's a gift. And trying to squelch it is beneath you. It's a weak move. You're smarter than that."

"Not really," I say for the first time in my life.

"You better get smart then. Remember, I fell in love with an artist too. I know what I'm talking about."

"But Dad followed you here." I think my argument is valid.

"What's your point?"

"He was the artist that sacrificed so you could pursue *your* path."

"And why? Because my big break had presented itself and I needed to take it. He didn't minimize the opportunity just because it wasn't his. He didn't say no because it was inconvenient. When I got the fellowship, it was a big deal. If I didn't take it, there were many that would have been glad to take my place. Your dad had not made a name for himself yet. He could continue to sculpt wherever he landed."

"That's another point. He hadn't established himself as an artist yet. I have established myself as an attorney."

"Who are you kidding? I know you can work remotely. That card doesn't play."

"But Dad was young. That alone makes the difference."

"It still was a sacrifice to leave France and come to the United States. And it wasn't temporary. He gave up everything to be with me. For my dream to flourish. The familiar, his contacts, the closeness of his family, all of it. And it was the right choice, wasn't it? Because his dream didn't die. He just found it here with me."

I sit with the words for a few beats, then add, "If I'm being honest, I don't like all the men around her either."

Her eyebrows lift in surprise. "Confidence in yourself is the biggest aphrodisiac, son. I wouldn't do that jealousy angle if I were you."

We leave the conversation there, as Parish stands for a toast to his bride. But I'm a hundred miles away, considering my mother's sharp opinions. I would be sired by a brilliant mind.

. . .

Turning off the downstairs lights, I head for the stairs. It's only nine thirty, but bed sounds too good to pass up. The empty space where Maudie used to sleep is filled with memories. I know it's a process, and I just have to go through this stage, but fuck. It's hard. I find myself avoiding certain places and pictures, just to get through the day without feeling like shit. I miss the hell out of her.

As I climb the first step, lights from an approaching car flood the space. Dove. I know the sound of her car like I know the sounds of her steps. Moving to the front door, I open it and watch as she parks and gets out.

"Hi! Thought I'd surprise you!"

"Good. I was just heading upstairs. Now you can join me."

"Let's have ice cream."

She climbs the porch steps and I take her in an embrace. "How did the meeting go?"

"Good. We're all nervous about tomorrow. Except for Jimmy of course."

As we walk inside, I flip on the lights.

"Is that his M.O.?"

"Nothing ruffles his feathers. I'll get the ice cream," she says, heading for the kitchen.

It's a throwaway remark, but it pisses me off. So, the guy is cool under fire. That's probably because he's trying to show off for you. You don't see it, but I do. God, I hate this side of me.

"What time do you have to be at your parents' tomorrow?"

"They want us all there by eleven. You know, pictures and getting dressed together. All the usual things."

"That's going to be so fun. I figure to get to the reception around four. That's not so bad, right?"

"Do whatever you need to. I'll fill the time avoiding dancing and eating shrimp. I'll most likely be drunk by the time you arrive."

She laughs, but I don't. I am one hundred percent serious. And completely over this week.

17
Dove

"Don't look like you're about to take a shit!" Deborah says, watching our images on the screen.

Oscar's shoulders relax and he shakes out his hands. I adjust the curl laying over my shoulder. Jimmy clears his throat. But ZZ? He stays where he is perched and doesn't change the serious expression. Nothing riles Tony much. He's cool under fire.

It was my idea to turn the camera and see how we look sitting together. Getting five people on one screen took a little effort and we don't have a lot of wiggle room. None of us wanted to be in separate locations. There is strength in numbers.

We are practicing being calm and somewhat collected, in advance of our Zoom call with Arthur. I may die of anticipation before it happens. The notes made lay out of the camera's range in case our minds go blank. There is a real chance it could occur.

Deborah stretches her arms. "Don't worry. If you stumble, I'll jump in."

When the Zoom engages my heart squeezes its response.

Oscar makes a barely heard squeak of a sound. As we join the meeting Arthur's face appears, and he's eating an orange slice. His face is a little rounder than last time we saw each other. But he's dressed just as sharp as always. You never see Arthur wearing last year's offerings.

"Everyone here?"

"Hi, Arthur. We're all here just holding our breaths," I say chuckling.

Hope that didn't sound desperate.

"Who's that?" He identifies the one surprise guest.

"I'm Deborah Taylor, Montana's manager. Nice to meet you, Arthur."

A low grumble proceeds his response. "Yeah, hi. Well, there's been some movement. We may be a little further into the story than you realize. First of all, your recording of "Mined" isn't good enough for release."

What? An electric charge travels up and down my spine. And not in a good way. It shocks me.

"What exactly does that mean?" Jimmy says defensively.

"It means I want you to come to Nashville and record it in my studio," Arthur bites back. "We need to get the right mix, and this isn't it. But the song has legs. I'm certain of it."

I grab Jimmy's hand on one side of me and Tony's on the other. Both out of the scope of the camera. I'm white knuckling it and so are they.

"You're thinking of releasing it on your label?" Deborah asks.

"Maybe. At the very least you're getting another chance to convince me it's worth the bother. Do not fuck it up. Hear me, Dove?"

Do I hold back or respond honestly? No contest.

"It's true, I fucked things up for my bandmates and myself. And I acknowledge causing trouble for you. But Arthur, it was a moral choice."

"I don't give a shit. When your moral choices affect me or my business, that's when we are going to have a problem. Make them on your own time. Got it?"

"Got it."

I only have Nobel to consider. And I know without question if he needed me to care for him, I'd do the same thing all over again. There's no reason to mention that hypothetical though.

"Okay. I'm booking your session for next Thursday. Is that a problem for any of you?"

Five voices agree with his schedule without a pause. If we have to run to Nashville naked, we will. This is the moment.

"We will be there. Thank you for the opportunity," Deborah says with a calmness that masks excitement.

"Good. I'll have Maggie send you the details about where you'll be staying. We can talk about the future when you get here. Deborah, you and I are going to have a long conversation. For now, we have to see what Michael Angelica proposes."

"How did it start with him? Had he seen us?" I ask.

"Not until he heard your song. I was listening to it when he came in for a meeting."

"Was that intentional on your part?" Jimmy asks.

"It's all intentional, Jimmy."

That is who this producer is. I think we are about to be educated in the business of music. Hopefully the reputation that precedes him is accurate. Smart, a fighter for his clients, and fair unless you fuck him.

"I know Archangel's debut tour is coming up. So you think we are going to be offered opening act for ...?" Tony gets half a question out.

"Don't know." The sharp response quiets us all. "He wants to see you perform. He will be discussing that with you today. Here's a tip when dealing with him. One. He's on his own time. Do not rely on him being punctual about anything other than his performances or recording sessions. Two. He is a man of few words when it comes to anything other than his music. That he can write a book on. He doesn't give a rat's ass for his personal life. And he doesn't care about yours. So, don't get chatty. It will work against you."

Jimmy speaks first. "You don't have anything to worry about, Arthur. No chatty musicians or divas here."

"Even if we had earned the status, it's not who we are," I add.

"I've heard that a hundred times before. It doesn't impress me. Actions do. Just be mindful of the advantage you're being offered."

"Okay. And we want to thank you, Arthur. For the second chance," I say with genuine gratitude.

"Yeah. Just get your asses here and we will see how things play out. No promises."

The call ends and the screaming starts. We are out of our seats and hugging each other before any words are spoken. I'm jumping up and down with Jimmy. Oscar heads for the refrigerator and a beer.

"Oh my God!!!" I scream. "Is this happening?"

"It's happening. Maybe, as Arthur says," Deborah adds.

"What time is it?"

"Almost one fifteen."

"Oh shit. I'm going to get dressed for the wedding. I've got time. Come with me," I say to Deborah.

Jimmy gives me a look which I choose to ignore and move into the bedroom. Closing the door behind me, I quickly strip out of my summer dress. Shoes get kicked off.

"That went well, huh?" I say.

"Think we have a good chance at this. God, what if we get a record deal?"

I grab the royal blue beauty and step in. "I'm so excited I can hardly stand it!" I say, stepping into my heels.

I look in Grandma's wall mirror, and can almost hear her voice, 'You look beautiful, honey', she would say.

Deborah has a final comment.

"Stay calm and everything will fall into place. Michael Angelica is gonna love you, honey. Everybody does."

Somewhere Grandma is smiling.

It's 7:04, two minutes later than the last time I checked.

"Please quit looking," ZZ says.

"I can't help it. We could be here all night."

Jimmy stands and goes to the window. "This is bullshit. He could have texted."

Deborah answers behind closed eyes as she stretches out on the couch. "Quit thinking he is on your schedule. That doesn't concern the man. Get used to it."

That reminds me how late I am to the wedding. It's already three hours past my guesstimate. At four I texted Nobel with the update. His response sounded like he was pissed. Five words. *Get here when you can.* Am I reading too much into that? I'm not leaving though. I will stay here if I have to sleep in this dress, sitting in this position in front of the computer.

I've already taken the shoes off and had a bite to eat. The band is unusually quiet. 7:05. I hear a horn honk on the next street.

The screen beeps. Zoom call!

"Oh hell, get back here," Deborah calls to the crew scattered across the room.

Tapping on the icon, we join the meeting. The face of Archangel appears. Wow. Michael Angelica is every bit as stunning as he comes across in pictures. The long curly hair, the pillowed lips, green eyes. He does kind of look angelic with a devilish twist.

"Hello, darlin'," he says. "Sorry I'm late. You understand." It's said in a stream of consciousness, as statement not a question.

I center and jump into the conversation. "No worries. Nice to meet you, Michael. Let me introduce the band. This is..."

"No time, luv. I just want to say how much I dig Montana's vibe. Your sound is different. Jimmy, brother you have a remarkable falsetto."

"Thanks, man."

"Each of you shine. So do your songs. Arthur played the latest one for me and filled me in on your history."

"You've never seen us?"

"I've seen the YouTube videos. We need to get together and see if there's anything there. You coming to Nashville?"

Tony breaks in the conversation. "Yeah. We will be there next week."

"Good. I will be at the session with Arthur. I want to watch, listen, see what I can learn. Here's your chance to impress. I'll see you in Nashville. Do not bring any other people to the recording studio. I have to concentrate on the music. I don't want to be making nice with your wives or husbands, or best friends. Do we have that straight?"

"Of course. See you in..."

The words *Michael has left the meeting* appear on the screen.

"WTF?" Tony says.

They wear frozen expressions, like if they move a finger, it will all disappear.

"Who gives a fuck? Do you realize what just happened?" Deborah says reanimating.

"I know! Not what I expected. But damn, it's all good!" I say.

"He complimented my falsetto," Jimmy adds under his breath.

We break out in wild abandon, complete with congratulatory cheek kisses and a few tears. I take the proper amount of time enjoying what I hope becomes one of the best days of my life.

Shit. Shit. Shit. I get out of the car and hand the key to the valet. It took thirty minutes to get through traffic.

"Thanks," I say, anticipating being handed the ticket. Come on, guy!

I sprint toward the hotel entry. Almost four hours late. That's the bottom line.

"Dove!"

I hear my name called as I pass through the doors. Van and the bridesmaid he is paired with are heading in my direction. His tie is untied, her updo is down, and I detect a bit of a problem with her walking straight.

"Your boyfriend isn't here. You missed it, girl," Van slightly slurs.

"You just missed the bride and groom too! They took off for the honeymoon," the girl says.

"That's what we should do," Van says to the girl. "I mean have a honeymoon."

"We would have to be married to go on a honeymoon," she teases.

"Who made up that stupid rule?"

He wears a boy's smile and a man's intention. I bet that has worked beautifully for him. The girl links her arm in his.

"You should have seen Nobel on the dance floor with our aunt. He was drunk as shit."

"Really? On the dance floor?"

Van starts laughing. "I know! It's a ridiculous development. He looked like he was about to break something."

"Oh God. I guess I'll call him and see if he wants company. Okay see you two later," I say to the retreating figures. They are headed for the front desk. Of course.

"No you won't," Van chuckles.

I want to see where the reception was and if Aurora and Gaston are still here. There are people in the doorway and music playing.

Walking through the entry to the large reception room, I'm greeted by the gorgeous flower arrangements on every round table and small white lights making the room look enchanted. It's beautiful and well done. While I'm sorry I had to miss the party, I have no regrets about being present for my own life.

A hand raises through the dancers and calls me forward. Aurora. She and Gaston are dancing to the band's take on a Tony Bennett song. They look like the couple on a romance book cover. He wears a perfectly tailored tux and she a modern, chic gown in lavender. The high heels show off her still great looking long legs. I move toward them, snaking through the last of the never say die guests.

"Hello! Oh, he left, Dove."

"I know," I say, kissing them both on the cheek as they sway in place. "I spoke to Van. Was the wedding everything you hoped for? How did the bride and groom do?"

"It was perfect. Parish cried when he saw Scarlett come down the aisle," Gaston says. "My boys are not afraid of showing their emotions."

"Let's go to the table and talk," Aurora says, taking my hand and leading us off the dance floor.

"You look beautiful, honey. Nobel is missing out," Gaston adds. "He had too many champagnes and wanted to put himself to bed."

As we take our seats, Gaston grabs a flute and pours me a champagne. He serves his wife and himself too.

"Are congratulations in order?"

I look at Aurora with question in my eyes. "For what?"

"Nobel said you were having an important phone call today about your music. Did it go well?"

The fact this woman is asking about my life and career makes me feel seen. She gets it, without knowing the details. Or maybe she knows more than I think. Whatever. She is simply supporting me. It gives me hope for Nobel. After all, she raised him.

"It did," I say, not holding back the excitement. "It went really well. I hope your son considers it good news too."

"He will." She says it like it is a given.

"I don't know."

"I do."

Is this just maternal cheerleading, or does she understand him on a deeper level than I do?

"I hope you're right, Aurora."

I lay a hand on Gaston's. "You two did a great job of raising your children. I admire you."

"It was a privilege. With Aurora to keep them in line, we did all right."

"I was the law," she chuckles, "he was the one who encouraged rebellion of the troops."

"That's your artist sensibility, Gaston. It's part of my makeup too," I say.

"I really think the best way children grow up is with a little of both," Aurora adds. "We were lucky to have a creative thinker, and also the logical straight shooter."

I turn to Gaston. "May I ask you a personal question?"

"Those are the best kind."

"In the end, what made you decide to leave Paris and live a life you knew nothing about?"

He takes a sip of champagne and looks me in the eye. "It was amor. I knew when she walked into my life nothing would ever be the same." He takes his wife's hand and threads his fingers in hers. "No matter what the storm was, she was the oasis in the middle."

"Oh, Gaston. That's so lovely," she says, smiling at her husband.

"It's true. There was no argument great enough to stay there. Nothing that topped the one to be with her. Once we fell in love, that love had the final word."

"Oh, honey! Why the tears?" Aurora says, using the napkin to wipe my cheek.

I couldn't stop my eyes from welling. And if ever there was a time to show my cards, it's now.

"It's just that I'm not sure Nobel will make that same choice. And if he didn't my life would never be the same."

"Do you love him?" Gaston asks.

"Yes. I do."

"Then stay who you are. That's the woman he fell in love with. Have a little faith in its power to persuade."

As I leave the venue, Gaston's words repeat in my mind.

All the way from my place to Nobel's, I am sending texts. No response. That doesn't stop me. I want to think the best of him. It is ridiculous to think he wouldn't be happy for me. It's still early, he's most likely watching television and eating ice cream. Maybe being a little pissed off at me for missing the wedding. I just need to hold firm. I did nothing wrong.

Women are used to putting men first. It has been that way forever. And we've done it with a good attitude! All we ask now is for the same consideration. There is nothing wrong with being dedicated and driven. It is something we have honored and looked up to in men. And the women that have supported generations of men striving to succeed? It was expected.

    I pull onto the property and drive slowly to the front of the house. It's dark, although some light still remains in the sky. I can't see the bedroom window from here, so maybe he's there stewing. I park and get out, after sending one final text and a gif of a woman with a hot dog in her mouth. Maybe sex will calm us both down.

    Up the steps. I knock. And knock. I press the doorbell. His car gives it away. He's here. No doubt. This is getting tiring. I'm not about to stand here all night, begging entry. It's time to show him how serious I am and how I expect to be treated. Respect. That's what I want. I turn and walk away.

18
Nobel

Tires on gravel. I heard her car as it pulled away from the house. Something held me back from going to the door. It wasn't just anger. It wasn't payback. I was out of the shower. I could have wrapped a towel around me and made it downstairs. Time was not the issue.

I needed to think. And a clear head to do it. The shower brought things back in focus. Now bed is the place to be. Sliding between the sheets, my body relaxes for the first time tonight. I exhale the last twelve hours and try to process where I find myself.

I know what to do. Use logic. It never failed me before. Pick the problem apart. Never look away from the truth. Wait. First damage control. Just in case I'm still drunk and when I wake up in the morning realize I'm wrong. I'd be happy if it happened.

I need to send a text, saying I was showering when she came over. The cameras alerted me, but by the time I saw the clip, she was long gone. I should add we'll talk tomorrow. Okay, good. *Send.*

That buys time to think about what happened today. It

was a clear look to the future, and the view was not great. Today I was a guy in his forties alone at a wedding. Making small talk, dancing with my aunt. But tomorrow, and every day forward, I could spend the better part of my life in the same position.

If I stay in Montana, I will be the odd man out at every wedding and party. If I go to Nashville, she'll be working while I'm in a downtown condo contemplating my navel. The view out my windows, buildings and concrete instead of majestic trees and a flowing river. Even if I go, how much of Dove will be mine? How much will belong to everyone else?

I've tried convincing myself the odds of fame are not great. But that's bullshit. I think they are going to be successful, and it scares the shit out of me. Either I go with her, or I stay here and have a mostly long distance relationship. Long distance love. There's no good choice.

And I'm not even considering what would happen if they became more successful and toured. I wouldn't fit in as a groupie and that's what it would feel like. Following them around, living out of a suitcase, sounds like hell to me. Except for the being with her part.

Just the lack of privacy and solitude, the general noise of the lifestyle, would be hard to adapt to. My invisibility would be compromised. It would take time to adjust my work habits and create movable workspaces. There are a million pieces to this puzzle.

But I love her. She loves me. That argument holds a greater weight. Could we meet on some middle ground I cannot see right now?

She hasn't even responded to my text.

Don't think she buys the shower story, but I'm sticking to it.

"Pass the syrup," she says, reaching across the table of the hole in the wall diner.

I picked a quiet spot for breakfast, tucked against the hills on the edge of the city. Neither one of us are one hundred percent relaxed. I feel the imbalance. Never felt it before. Jumping into the problem seems the best way forward.

"So I was thinking of our predicament all night."

She looks me in the eyes and a seriousness appears. "What predicament is that?"

That sort of pisses me off.

"I think you know. How are we going to handle this long distance? I can't see me tagging along club to club and then hardly having your company."

Her fork is laid on the plate. She locks eyes with me and delivers the news.

"Nobel, it might be much worse than that."

Didn't expect that response.

"Meaning what?"

"Meaning if things work, we will cut a record. You haven't heard all the news yet, because *you were in the shower.* But there's more."

The way she says it is pointed and accusatory. She's right, but it doesn't stop me from not liking it.

"What?" I say.

"Archangel's lead singer is interested in us. Hopefully he likes what he hears when we go to Nashville next week. Are you familiar with the country band?"

"Well yeah. I'm not that old or out of the loop."

"Didn't say you were. It's just that their rise has been recent."

"What does that all mean? What does he have to do with you?"

"Not sure yet."

"You're going to Nashville for how long?"

"I don't know for sure. Arthur wants to rerecord "Mined" at his studio. That's huge in itself. He wouldn't put the money in if he didn't think it was going to pay off."

"Congratulations. I'm happy for you, Dove. You deserve the recognition."

As much as it is hard to admit, what I said was the truth. Minus one thing. Happy for her, unhappy for me.

"But there's more." She doesn't break eye contact.

I am not going to like this.

"If it turns out the record is as good as Arthur believes, it will be released under his label. Maybe we will be signed. If so, it will be important to stay so we can write and record more songs there. Be close to the label."

I lean back in the booth and take a breath.

"Wow. This is a lot to take in. Moving to Nashville for good?"

"It's a probability if things go our way."

I huff a response, not certain why I factor so little into the story she's telling.

"What about us?" I lay it all on the line.

"What about us? There are choices to make. You can come with me. We're in love, Nobel. I can't bear to think of you being here, and me being in Tennessee alone."

"Obviously you can."

I hurt her with that sharp response. But it was accurate. I got used to making my point in law school. Identify the hole in the argument if it can be found. Tears fill her eyes and at first I do nothing to stop them. I'm hurt too. Just because I'm not crying is no indication of the depth of the wound. The silence is thick, and it sits between us. I reach for her hand, and she gives it to me without hesitation.

Our eyes are almost begging to see hope in the face of the

person across the table. Some crack in the wall that would say there is room for compromise.

"I understand what you are feeling. It's a lot," she says in low tones.

I play with her delicate fingers, so soft against my hand. "I'd love to be like you, Dove. But I'm set in my ways. And I never fool myself that I'm anything different. It sucks because I actually wish I could be."

She leans in. "But what about how we all morph into something new, whether it's on purpose or not. Life changes us all the time."

"I wish it would change me now."

Her hand raises to my cheek and it's so tender a gesture.

"I don't want you to change. I think you're perfect. But what I do want is for you to be the man who, in spite of being uncomfortable, offers up his discomfort to be with the woman he loves."

I don't know what to say. There is a logic to that, and it feels uncomfortable knowing I may not be capable.

Her hand drops, and she continues. "And in return, I promise you the same. There will come a day when you need me to stand by you. And I will. It would be a given."

I let her words settle in my mind, where I pick them apart. My heart already knows the truth. But my mind. That fucker fights till the end.

"Your career demands so much of you, Dove. I understand that. But it would demand things of me too. That's something that seems unscalable."

She sighs before presenting her final argument.

"Great things seldom come from comfort zones, Nobel. It's all just words before you are asked to do it. The proof is in the doing. I *have* stood with those I love and been happy with the choice. With me, love wins out. Over music and career. Over every fucking thing. It's you who doesn't see it in yourself, and I'm not sure I see it in you either."

"That's harsh," I say, feeling the sting.

"Yeah, it is."

We finish breakfast, passing the time trying to ignore where we find ourselves. Small talk seems odd. One click off the norm. All of a sudden, it doesn't flow at the same pace. But we keep at it because the sound of silence is heartbreaking. Our deepest selves are exposed. The chink in my armor, her sense of self.

I have five days to figure out how to bend. And if I don't, I will find out what it feels like to break. *Asshole*, I say to myself.

On the way out of the diner, our better angels reach for each other's hand.

The days pass with a quickness I anticipated. Time runs out, as it always does. No matter how much we want to hold on to a day or a moment, it dissolves and reappears as the past. Day by day you think nothing has changed. Then you look back and see it all has. I feel nearly dead. It's all about her leaving now.

It has become increasingly clear that this is no false start to Montana's real rise. The phone calls and Zoom meetings have increased with each day. Jimmy and Dove are writing furiously. At least I was able to contribute some general legal advice on a few points when they asked for my input. It was a short high though. A shallow contribution.

The producer is interested beyond what he is saying. Just his mention of contracts and timelines tells me he has already made up his mind. He's a bit too obvious to hide the fact. Think he's afraid someone else will scoop them up. And it hasn't escaped Dove or her bandmates. Rightfully so, they each are charged with the reality of the situation. This is the end of their long beginning.

It becomes clearer with every day that passes. I am about to lose my mountain girl to the world. I hate that she tries to hide her excitement. But she does. The natural joy has been tapped down for my fucking benefit. That truth can't be ignored. Am I becoming the one thing in Dove's life that tries to hold her back? It would be fucked up to quiet the nightingale's song. That is a horrible thought about myself.

Now it's our last night together before the flight to Nashville in the morning. I don't want to see a clock or have any idea of the time. All I know is that this could be, and probably is, the last of us as we were. After tomorrow she becomes something new. Damn. I love the old us. Why can't things ever stop evolving when you get it right?

We've been laying in each other's arms for an hour, watching the light from the full moon. It's visible through the open window. There is a sadness to the image and scene. Maybe everything from here on will have that melancholy feel. I know it's my mindset, but I don't see it changing. Despite efforts to be a better man, I know myself. Dove said it early on as a compliment. Now it has become my undoing.

All I can do is try to take this one step at a time. Don't live it before it happens. I've told myself that all day. So far it hasn't stuck beyond the time it took to think. Consequently, I die a hundred deaths, like all cowards do. To erase the thought, I kiss the top of her head and hold her closer.

She meets my gaze.

"I'm bad with words right now, Dove. I hope you're good at reading eyes."

I don't wait for the answer. It's difficult to stop thinking of the real possibility I'm about to lose her. The reality sucks. She doesn't know how slow the moments go when we are apart. If we end up living in different places permanently, time will stop.

"Kiss me," she says softly.

We come together gently at first. Her silky skin. Blonde hair falling over my chest and shoulders. The sweet breath and taste of her mouth. The shape of her breasts. I try to memorize it all. To make some facsimile in my mind, that can be called up at will when I don't have her next to me. When she becomes the world's pleasure and not mine. But tonight's for us. I throw off the covers.

"I'm going to give you a massage. Roll on your stomach."

"Oh, yes please. Want to put a towel down?"

"No. I don't care if it stains the sheets."

"Let's have music," she says. "Alexa! Play Dove's playlist."

The smooth sounds of Chris Botti's trumpet sets a mood. "What Are You Doing the Rest of Your Life?" Seems weirdly appropriate.

"Now just relax."

Lifting her long hair she tucks it over a shoulder. Giving me an all access pass. I take the bottle of oil and squeeze it over her back, between her shoulder blades and down her spine. My hands begin a subtly sensuous journey starting at the shoulders and neck. Kneading soft flesh in a slow steady rhythm.

"That feels sooo good," she says, face to pillow.

I wish she could feel what she does to me. It's fucking unbelievable.

I move to her beautiful arms, taking a journey up and down the length of them. After a while the tension starts to release and her hands relax. Sliding over the shoulder, then round and around, my fingers reach toward her breast. A little closer each time. I take her wrist and gently bend the arm behind her back at the waist. Now I lift the shoulder and reach for the mound of a perfect breast, letting my hand cup and massage the entire orb.

With each pass I linger longer on the nipple, tickling it at first, flicking the tip. Pinching. It's hot that she likes it.

"Baby." Her voice is low and sounds like desire.

My dick responds by standing. I give it a few strokes, even though it makes not mounting her torture.

One beautiful brown eye opens. "Do all your customers get this treatment?"

"You're my only client. You get all the treatments."

"You're going to get a huge tip for that."

"You're going to get a huge tip for this," I say, pulling on an aroused nipple.

She giggles, and it makes me harder. I move to the other shoulder and breast. Nipple. Nipple. Nipple. I could fucking come playing with her tits. I'm hard as fuck. With hands on her narrow waist, I press my palms into her lower back and move up and out. Over again. More.

"Ahhh."

I go lower. What a great ass. It rises with my touch, like she is offering a gift. I want her to wait for it. To feel the pull. Yeah. I want her to fucking want it. I'm gonna fuck that. That ass and pussy is a fuckin' feast.

"Let me see!"

Legs spread with the command. The woman is a mistress when it comes to the tease. As master, I'm going to return the favor. With each movement I'm a millimeter closer to the holy land. Fingers finding buried treasure. I want to smell that thing. Smell her sex on my mouth. Just the thought sends a bolt to my balls.

I bury my face in between silky legs and breath in the scent of her. It makes me want to come. She knows what I'm doing and likes it. There is this rawness to the woman. I love that she is so open. Makes me want to fuck her all day long.

The pink lips. They're calling me. Oh yeah there's the clit. It's peeking out of the hood. Sucking that tiny center of the universe gets me hard. Even her asshole is asking for attention. It's sitting there daring me to finger it.

My breathing. The heartbeat. My dick. I want her *bad*.

A slow, intimate rubbing begins. At first fingers just grazing the edges of her lips. Then taking more. Going deeper. I part them and look at the wet heart of everything. I want her so fucking much. Lifting to her knees, I'm invited to have a closer look. Moonlight highlights the glistening oil on the roundness of her ass, on the curve of the spine. She squeezes her pussy, knowing what it does to me to watch as lips tighten then release. The sight is mine alone.

I step back and squeeze oil in my hands. Rubbing it over my torso and arms. On my thighs. Dove's head turns. The blonde hair wild and sexy as shit. She watches like a caged female lion waiting for me to mount her. I grab ahold of my raging dick and climb on the bed behind her. Uh huh. Like this, baby.

19
Dove

His cock. It's a granite rod. He knows what he wields, and comes to me gently. A man, considering the softness of a woman. There's a control threatening to be lost. It makes me wet knowing he struggles to contain himself. That is the sexiest, the very sexiest thing.

Like at any moment he might lose it and take me with or without permission. Although my ass in his face is invitation enough. The strength in his body sits behind every soft touch, but much closer with the not so soft ones. I fucking love when it hurts just a little. You're good at the art, baby. Having that big cock guarantees my satisfaction. It hurts so good. *Fuck me. Fuck me.*

With a hand on my cheek, he rubs the silk covered steel tip against my lips. I hear the labored breathing and sense the sexual storm contained inside him. It threatens to break the hurricane shutters and rip off the roof. Ignoring anything that dares get in its way. But my storm rages too. I'm pulling down all barriers and letting it run free. Come with me, baby.

The tip. He teases without mercy. It feels really good

though. My pussy is on fucking fire. Slick juices allow the glide. I want more. My back arches and I press my pussy into him, asking without words.

"Take it," his low voice commands.

There's no hesitation. Not on his part or mine. The cock enters me in a slow, but unstoppable drive. My body becomes electric. Cells and atoms dance to his beat. Every bit of me, a part of him. That makes him part of me. The slow, rolling motion. God yes. You are a master at the grind. This is fucking awesome. *He's not going to choose you.*

The shocking thought pushes its way into my mind. The ground shifts. Uninvited, it threatens any remaining hope. It goes right to my heart. I want to get back. Trying to ignore the intruder, I concentrate on being in the moment.

"That's good, baby," I say.

I hear myself speak. It sounds like someone else is talking. Not because I don't mean the words, but because I am not wholly here. There's a sense of going through the motions. While part of me, hidden deep inside, can't stop crying for us. It's impossible to forget what I know. Or stay in the mood to be having sex.

I feel we are dissolving by the minute. He isn't going to make the right decision. I know it. That's what takes center stage. Even this intimacy that has meant so much, is changing. *Where did we go?*

"I love fucking you," he says between deep thrusts.

But there is something in the voice that sounds like sadness. A stillness leaking out with the joyful words. He needs to be processing the same things. He's just doing a better job at hiding it. I try to use my body to convince myself and Nobel that I am still here. Getting lost in his sex has never been a difficulty. Until now.

I give it my all, pumping against him faster and harder. This is the first time I have ever tried to rush it. Before tonight, things were different. My orgasms were built with time, to make the explosions last. But I know tonight, if I just let it play out, I will never get there. Plus, a tightness builds in my throat. *Oh shit! No!* A heavy tear courses down my face. Then another.

Nobel meets my pace and grabs the sides of my waist tighter, to pull me to him with every thrust.

Thankfully it doesn't take long for him to get to the point of no return. Then I do something I vowed never to do with a man, and especially not with this man. I fake it.

While groans and sounds of orgasm spill from his mouth, I'm doing my best to mimic orgasming. It's not easy. Sounds false start to finish. Think I overdid it. But I needed to let this out. We slow to the final pumps and grunts. I end with an obligatory *ohhhhhhh*. It's relief. I can wipe my eyes now.

As he separates from me and kisses my backside, I'm repositioning myself against the headboard.

"That was great," I say, fluffing a pillow behind my back.

He just looks at me. Studying my face for answers to unspoken questions.

He stays in the kneeling position at first.

"Did you come?"

"What? Yes! Didn't you hear me?" I say, going for genuine. But it was a little shrill. I heard it. Sounded like a lie.

He climbs to where I lay and joins me.

"I heard you. It seemed different. Just my mood I guess."

Taking his hand, I kiss it and hold it against my face. Neither of us suggest we keep fucking. This was the shortest sexual escapade we have ever had.

"It's been such a long week. Maybe I was a little distracted. But I got there. And as usual, you were perfect. It felt wonderful," I lie, covering the next gap in conversation with a deep kiss.

Time is so unkind. It persists in passing, bringing me closer to leaving.

Then fate delivers a final blow. I see a vision. The woman that appeared by the river, while Nobel held the child, is standing behind him on the porch of this house. The trees and flowers tell a story too. It's late in the day in early spring. Their backs are to me, looking out to the vista. I am nowhere to be seen.

"You understand, right?" Nobel says, looking for the Uber driver.

"Yeah, I do. This is bad enough."

He won't be coming to the airport and it was the right decision. He sets the suitcase and carry-on on the porch. I have dropped any pretense of normalcy. I'm over pretending I don't know what is going to happen.

"Let's sit out here and wait," he says, taking a chair.

I pull one close and take my place. We automatically braid fingers. Maybe it's for the final time. If I have to stay in Nashville and he decides to stay here. How could we go back to another kind of relationship? Apart when we have the ability to be together. I couldn't do that.

"Remember to watch yourself," he says as he always does when we are apart. "Hotels can be dangerous when you're a single woman alone."

"Okay, Dad."

He catches himself and chuckles. "I do sound like that. Can't help it."

"So I'm going to call you every night. I'll keep you posted as soon as I know what's happening."

The sound of an approaching car reaches our ears. We lock eyes.

"I'm wishing you every good thing that could possibly happen for you guys. Hitch your wagon to that star, Dove."

He wants me to believe him and I do. I also believe it won't change him. Both things are true.

The Uber driver pulls in front of the house. He gets out to put the luggage in. My stomach tightens.

"Morning."

"Morning. Thank you."

Nobel surrounds me with his embrace and holds me close. Here we are.

"I love you. You know that, right?" He says it like a goodbye. That's what I hear.

"I love you too. Always."

I separate, look deep in the still pool of his green eyes and stay silent. What else is there to say or do to make him understand what love requires?

I walk down the steps but turn back as I stand by the open door.

"Don't forget us, Nobel."

I slide into the back seat. "I'm going to the airport. United."

My eyes stay looking ahead. There's no looking back now.

Music Row is just southwest of downtown Memphis. "Musica", the forty-foot bronze statue, is the centerpiece of the roundabout. It gives me a thrill as it comes into view. Nine disrobed male and female figures dance in a circle atop a base of limestone boulders.

Beautiful tree-lined streets. Homes with wrap around porches that have been turned into recording studios. The best and the brightest, the most famous have recorded here. It looks unassuming. It is anything but. One would never know Dolly Parton or Garth Brooks made some of their most famous recordings in these buildings. Even Elvis Presley. So cool.

I expected big buildings. Bet most people do. Glamour and glitz seemed a given in my fantasy of the place. Instead, it is an architecturally unimpressive spot with a few signs pointing out where musical history has been made. Some would be underwhelmed. Not me. After all, fancy or not, this was the birthplace of country music.

The limo and driver Arthur sent to bring us to Studio James pulls into the underground parking of a nondescript three story building. This is the well-respected studio? It's currently recording albums for three top of the charts artists. We did our digging and found out it's not only contract players that use the studio, but independent artists do as well. The reputation proceeds the engineers who mix the tracks and the studio musicians that play here. Not to mention the touted skills of the producer and his team. All working together at the top of their game. No surprise they would be in demand.

"I have to take a shit," ZZ says, apropos of nothing.

"Just fucking hold it."

"I'll hold it in your fucking hands," ZZ comes back.

But it doesn't piss Tony off, in fact it breaks the tension, and we start laughing.

"You'll have time. We're a little early."

Jimmy leans in and addresses the group.

"Do you think this is normal?" he whispers, gesturing to the vehicle we find ourselves in. "Does everyone arrive in a limo?"

"Who cares? I'm just going to enjoy the ride," Oscar adds.

"I'm thinking he wouldn't send a car if he had any idea the music wasn't going to pay off," ZZ says.

"Or if he didn't think he'd sign us."

As the car pulls up to the elevators and stops, I add one more thought. "Don't jinx it! Let's just take it step by step."

"What floor do we go to?" Jimmy asks.

"It's all Studio James. Just walk inside. There will be someone there to guide you."

"Thanks, man."

"Good luck to you," the driver says, turning to us with a smile.

"Thank you!"

Obviously, he has delivered other overly excited and nervous artists to this underground foundation of hopes and dreams. We share one thing, regardless of styles and genres. To reach this level, music has held a holy place in our lives.

It's sweet that he understands.

We pile out and straighten our clothes as the limo pulls away. Even ZZ checks his zipper. Don't think I have ever seen him in formal wear. The newer jeans and long-sleeved shirt qualify.

Getting in the elevator we meet each other's eyes. Every single one of us aware of the weight of the moment. The first floor button is pushed. Jimmy lets out a long sigh.

"I'm so fucking nervous," Tony says, fiddling with his bracelets.

"Me too," I add.

"I have to shit." ZZ states the more serious problem.

The door slides back to an understated small lobby. There are no gold records or awards on the espresso colored walls. Just modern furniture and upscale lighting.

The woman sitting at the modern desk at the far end is speaking with... Oh shit! It's Marley Mantley. Country's latest golden goose. Her writing is so good. Walking forward, it feels like I have cement in my shoes. She turns with our approach.

"I'm just leaving. I'm boring my friend here to death. That's a cool dress!" She holds out my arms for a better view.

Now to pretend I'm perfectly used to speaking with a star.

"Thanks!"

I go blank. She must be used to people spazzing out and comes to my rescue.

"I'm Marley."

Her hand reaches for mine.

"Yes. Of course. I'm sorry," I say, spinning my index finger around my temple. As if she didn't figure out I'm crazy already. "I'm Dove. We're Montana, this is Jimmy and Tony. Oscar and ZZ."

She makes eye contact with each person and they exchange the pleasantries.

"Oh! You're the ones who booked my favorite room tomorrow."

She raises a fist in a comical stance.

"We did?" Jimmy says.

Now I watch her put something interesting together.

"Or maybe someone booked it for you?"

None of us know what to say, but she expertly reads the room and puts what she knows together.

"There's talk about your song. But don't say it came from me," she says, walking away with a backwards wave. "Good luck, y'all."

I feel my nails digging into Tony's bare arm.

"Ow! Fuck, Dove. I need this one!"

"Sorry. Oh my God, that just happened!"

"We're here to see Arthur James," Jimmy says to the young, hip receptionist.

I expect a nonchalant attitude, but she surprises me.

"Hi. Welcome! Mr. James is ready to see you. Through the double doors to your right."

It's like a scene in a television show. The naïve talent stands nervously, ten steps away from another world.

"Tell me about it," Nobel says across the miles.

It's early. Watching the morning sunlight stream through the blinds of the hotel room, I'm still in bed.

"Oh it was everything we have ever dreamed about. Baby, I almost started crying."

"That's so exciting. What did he say?"

I sit up against the headboard and cross my legs.

"He said our song is really good. My little songwriter heart practically stopped. We were all like that. But today we're going to rerecord it. It's so exciting to think we are going to be in this famous, first class studio, with the pros. The mixing, the equipment, the guidance. It's all so far above what we have experienced before."

"What about that Archangel guy? Did you meet yet?"

"No. He'll be there this afternoon. We are nervous about impressing him, but if Arthur's right, it's already a done deal."

"Sounds like this Arthur is a pretty straightforward guy. What's your general impression?"

"That's exactly what he is. At least that's how it seems now. He was cool with Deborah, who he immediately figured out. She didn't try to oversell her talents, and he didn't undervalue her good sense and natural abilities. He wasn't talking down to her, just because her exposure to this level is nil."

"That's impressive."

"I think he reads people really well."

"It sounds like you are on your way. I'm so happy for you, Dove."

"Are you? For real?"

"For real. Call me after your session. I'll be waiting to hear the good news."

A genuine wish is in there somewhere. But I know sadness sits behind it. The timber in the voice and the rhythm of the statement is skewed. I don't think anyone but me would notice. It isn't his natural joy. The sense of happiness coming in waves has stilled. He's trying though. He's trying so hard.

20
Nobel

It's the pivot point. I'm a little drunk, but not enough to miss the indelible writing on the wall. Here we are. Everything has happened fast. She wouldn't agree with that take. After all, they worked their asses off for years already. I'm only judging from my first look at her. Then to now is just a moment. I down the last swallow of whiskey and pour a refill. That's the most I've moved in two hours. Sitting in the dark living room, watching the sun and my hopes fade is exercise enough.

It's going to take the rest of the bottle to stand by my decision. Why prolong the inevitable? Being under the influence when making a decision is pretty stupid. I don't have the courage to do it another way. Rip the band-aid off and be done with it. It would be cruel to prolong telling her. This way, she can be finished with the personal drama. I wonder if any of her friends sense she is struggling with our relationship? Do they see a difference in behavior or mood?

I bet they hate seeing her not fully present. Am I paying enough attention to my boyfriend seems a teenager's problem, not a woman's. It would be cruel having to constantly be checking my emotional temperature, as if I was lacking the confidence of a man. Oh God. I'd hate doing that to us. We would lose the spontaneity. That would be the first thing that would happen.

In a matter of two weeks, every fucking thing has changed. Recording "Mined", signing with James Records, and beginning to record another song that was written a few years back. She said Arthur is acting like he's discovered buried treasure. He's right. She wept when she told me.

That Archangel dude is the unknown. He hasn't offered anything concrete yet, but she says talk of Archangel's tour in November has come up a few times. She thinks he is waiting for the release of "Mined" next month before he decides. If he knows what's good for him and his band, he'd grab ahold of Montana now.

There was barely a moment when I wasn't thinking about her these last weeks. About us. About them. It rolls around my mind on a loop, unmerciful in its persistence. If it happens now, before the effect of fame, what would it be like after?

Asked and answered. Last night when I was just about to say I love her, the call from Michael Angelica interrupted. Not that I'm jealous of the guy in the general sense of the word. It's just that there doesn't seem to be a space for us. Not one that shuts out every other demand. And that's what I would turn into. A demand of her time and attention.

What kind of life would that be? That may be oversimplification, but it reduces to that. The realization makes up my mind. Has everything been illusion, not magic? A man's attempt at believing love exists? Bullshit. I love her and I will *never* deny the truth. Trouble is, I love her enough to let her fly. I'm going to tell her that when she calls. Yeah, that's what I'll do. Leaning my head back on the chair, I put the drink down and close my eyes. Just for a minute. Maybe I can stop thinking.

. . .

Fuck. I peek out of one sleepy eye. It's dark outside. At least an hour or two has passed and my back feels like shit for sitting crooked. In my stupor, posture didn't factor into the equation. It fits though. This has been one clusterfuck of a day. Nothing has changed, except for a desire to be drunker.

The cell sounds. Grabbing the phone with one hand and the whiskey bottle with the other, I tap the name and take a long pull.

"Hello?" Dove says, wondering where the fuck I am. Why I'm not speaking.

"I'm here. Right fucking here." It is said with a slight slur I hadn't noticed before.

There is a pause before her response. "Are you drinking? You sound like it."

"I am. Good deduction, Sherlock."

Didn't realize it would come out with an attitude.

"Maybe I should wait to tell you the news," she says with an attitude of her own.

"Tell me now. How much worse could it be?"

The pit bull in her voice bites back. "Worse? What news have I given you that was bad?"

I chuckle and within the sound is the desire to tell her what I really want to say. This is the spot to lay it out. I'm drunk and angry enough to pull it off.

"The list is too long. Let's just get to today's headline."

She pauses, and I ask again.

"Tell me what spectacular thing happened to you today."

"No. You don't deserve to know, and I don't deserve this bullshit attitude."

I take another swig of whiskey.

"See. I already stole your thunder. This isn't going to work, Dove. For either of us."

There's a long pause before my words reach her head and heart.

"What."

It is not a question she asks. The realization of what I'm saying wounds her. And for just a moment it almost makes me reconsider. Hurting her is torment, and I am completely aware that is what I'm doing. But better now than later when it will hurt more. It is said hope springs eternal. But false hope is a dead thing. It's worse than the ugly truth and only prolongs the inevitable.

She whispers, "Don't you love me?"

My heart sinks.

"It's because I love you."

Silence. Then the phone goes dead. Along with myself.

Day two of this new reality begins as expected. I wake up feeling like a pile of shit. Sunlight through the windows is harsh on bloodshot eyes. I need to stop drinking today. As soon as the thought leaves me, I eye the bottle. No. What time is it? Checking my cell, I skim by the eleven thirty numbers and go directly to messages. None from her.

Drool has dried on the side of my mouth, and the headache is bad. But the urge to piss worse. Standing slowly, I feel the result of sleeping on the couch with a jacket as a pillow. My clothes are twisted and wrinkled. For the first time in my life, I feel old. Not sure what to blame, last night's bed, or last night's drama.

"Fuck."

The bathroom seems a mile away, but halfway there, Dove appears in my mind. It's done. I made it clear. Hope I was kind. Not sure I was. A fuzzy memory of her wounded surprise tells me the answer. Should I text and see how she's feeling today? Don't be a passive aggressive ass. Of course, you shouldn't. I cut the cord, severed the ties, now I need to live it. Funny how those euphemisms both involve a knife and a wound disguised as good sense when someone has too much influence.

I drop my pants and release the flaccid hound. Images of her. Awww. Relief. Even when I'm pissing, she takes center stage. There's a persistent nudge poking my consciousness. A voice trying to get my attention and point out the obvious. *You are an asshole. You are.*

A shake and a zip later, I head for the kitchen. Better eat something. Maybe it will fill the hole in my life.

Ring! The doorbell sounds annoying. I check the phone and access the front porch camera. Shit it's Aargon. I don't feel like talking. But fuck, the shutters are open, and the curtains drawn back. I can't get out of it.

Walking to the door I see him looking inside. Watching as I approach.

"Hey," I say, opening the door.

I must look bad, because his eyebrows knit together and his mouth tightens.

"What happened to you? You look like shit."

He follows me into the kitchen, waiting for an answer.

"Nothing. I had a few too many drinks last night."

"What happened?" He doesn't take no for an answer.

I load the coffee maker while filling in the blanks.

"I broke it off with Dove."

There it is wrapped in a nutshell.

He moves closer, to have eye contact.

"What are you talking about? Why?"

"Because it's not going to work. I don't want to talk about it, okay?"

"No. It isn't okay. I want to know."

I turn and lean against the counter. "Coffee?"

The disgust on his face tells me I'm in for it.

"Quit fucking around, Nobel. Was it her idea?"

"No! Why are you saying that? It was me. A hundred percent me."

"Did she cheat?"

"No."

"Did you get tired of the sex?"

"No, that didn't happen," I say pointedly.

"Does she bore you?"

"There's nothing boring about the woman."

"Well what then?"

I take a few beats before telling the story.

"I told you about rerecording the song."

"Yeah."

"It went well. Better than they imagined. They have to relocate to Nashville."

"That's great."

"Is it? For them. But for me, it means giving this all up. Changing everything about my life. They are going to be based out of Nashville, probably go on tour, etcetera. I'd be the groupie."

He looks at me and I know what's coming.

"I don't get it. I thought you two were in love."

"We are. Were. Are."

"Don't be so shortsighted, brother. You can't stay The Invisible Man forever, just because it's comfortable to hide."

"You don't understand."

"I understand more than you do."

"Really? Are you the grand wizard of love?"

As soon as the words leave my mouth, I regret saying them. His eyes show the sadness he lives with.

"I might be. At least I'm the wizard of losing it. That makes a man an expert in appreciating what can't be replaced."

"Sorry, Aargon. I'm a dick."

"Don't be a stupid one. I know what it's like to have it and lose it. I wouldn't wish it on anyone, let alone my brother."

I sit with the thought.

"I can hardly believe you would actually choose it, Nobel."

I have nothing to add. This headache is pounding like a jackhammer. Aargon sees the mood, and switches topics.

"You know it's Mom and Dad's anniversary tomorrow, right?"

"Shit. No. I'm not in the mood for a party."

"Well, you lucked out. They're going to spend the weekend in Memphis. I guess that was where they spent their wedding night. I just thought you might want to call them before they take off."

"Thanks," I say, pouring a cup of coffee. "Want one?"

"No. I have to go. But I hope you're going to give the whole Dove thing another look. I think you're fucking up the best thing that ever happened to you. For *nothing*."

"My life is not nothing."

"It will be if you let her go. Take it from me."

Three hours and a million reflections later, I'm trying to put on the best face I can.

"Happy anniversary, you two lovebirds."

Thank God for FaceTime. The parental units are not the most tech savvy duo.

"Darling, thank you for remembering."

"Why are you looking like that? Are you sick?" My father always gets to the point.

"No. Just a headache. So you're going to recreate your wedding night I hear."

They chuckle with the thought.

"Well, there may be a small change here and there.

Nothing your mother will notice. I'm still the virile Frenchman I was then."

But their laughter tells a slightly different story. She touches his cheek, looks into his eyes and smiles.

"Gaston, you have only improved with the years."

He chooses to believe the lie and offers a little kiss.

"So what's happening in your life? How's Dove?" he asks, pretending innocence.

I call bullshit. I am sure Aargon has told the interested parties about my…stupidity. I'm only using his word.

"I know you know," I say, cutting to the chase.

Their expressions change. Both begin talking over the other.

"What are you thinking?"

"Call her and say you made a mistake!"

"Stop."

It is as if I muted the screen. They quiet and wait for me to explain myself.

"I had to cut it off now. If I had waited it would have ruined the best time of her life."

"Darling, don't you know you're the best time of her life?"

The very thought that could be true, makes a compelling argument.

"That's what love is, son."

My mother adds another thought. "Think about what you are doing, Nobel. You're bringing logic and reasoning to the fight, and they are seriously outmatched by your heart."

"As your father, I tell you I see it all over your face. You're miserable without her."

"If you really love her, you'll be with her. That's it. Whether it's on her playing field or yours."

"And nothing will stop you. Not even your own stupid missteps," my father adds with emphasis.

I don't have a witty retort. Hell, I can't even think of a

rebuttal. And that's the second time someone called me stupid in two days. That must mean it's true.

"I have to get off. I have a client to talk with," I lie, and they know it. "Have a wonderful anniversary. Love you guys."

"Go, go! Take care of business," my mother sends a not so subtle message.

"Thanks for calling, son! We're going to check back in a few days. See if you came out of your coma."

They do not wait for me to argue with the brutal assessment. They sign-off.

All day long, I work to be in another state of mind. I catch up with the business that has piled up in the last weeks. I make myself a good lunch. I put on background music to work by, but that was a mistake. Everything reminded me of Dove. Whether it was rock or classical, she came into my mind and made the music make sense. I couldn't handle that.

I wanted to turn off the phone when my siblings wouldn't leave me alone. Word has spread. The Invisible Man has gone into hiding again and they're not having it. So basically, I'm ignoring them all. Decline, Decline, Decline.

The house has become lonely. No Dove, no Maudie, just a stillness that has nothing to do with serenity.

So, I sit on the porch watching the sun go down. Wondering where home went. Thoughts have nowhere to go but to her.

Every argument has been made. I've used all the tools at my disposal to rationally stand my ground, and they are worthless. I have painfully turned every stone. Against all that she is, my weak arguments fail. It is a proverbial wall I have hit and Dove stands on the other side waiting. There is no going around. If I want to get to her, I need to destroy the barricade I built in life, brick by brick.

"Fuck me," I say to the trees.

I'm left to become a new man or left to return to what I was before. Shit. Why would I want to be him? Yeah, I was happy enough, and the routine in my life felt like satisfaction. Now I know too much. Her chaos has become my calm. Besides, the man I was is gone for good, whether I go or not. It is impossible to forget who I became loving her.

I stand. Love may be a mistake. But it's the one worth making.

21

Dove

"I'm not going to ask again if you're sure."

"Good."

Deborah watches as I point to the turnoff for the airport.

"Even though it makes me nervous you won't be back in time."

That's the real fear. And I understand the hesitation. It looks like I am risking *everything*. Like I will let the brass ring slip from my hands and therefore the hands of my friends.

"No need to worry. It's going to work out. I get back at noon tomorrow, you're going to pick me up, or us up, and no one will be the wiser."

"Yeah. That's what your ticket says. But what if there's bad weather or mechanical issues?"

"Then I will wait for the next flight. We have two days."

We get in the line of cars inching toward drop off for American Airlines.

"Not really. You have a day and a half till we meet with the attorney. Your bandmates would think it odd if you weren't there Monday morning."

"If worse comes to worst, I can say I'm sick. It would buy me a little time. But that isn't going to happen!"

"I don't know. Tony and Jimmy are suspicious something is up. They think it's weird you're staying in, the first few days you've had off in weeks."

I feel Deborah's nerves coming to the surface. Her face is pinched, and she's hardly blinked in the last minute. I am perfectly calm. It comes from knowing this is meant to be. Not that I had a vision, or any kind of premonition. It's because what I am doing feels right.

She pulls over against the curb.

"Okay, there is no talking you out of this, Dove. Just, no matter how this turns out, whether he's happy to see you or not, get your ass back by tomorrow night."

"I will. Promise."

"And don't let Arthur know you're anything but perfectly happy. Fuck. This is a bad idea."

I look her in the eyes. "No it isn't. It's the best idea I've ever had."

She gives up trying to talk me out of it, a deep sigh the final comment.

If I didn't make a stand for us and let Nobel know I'm a fighter, I deserve to be without him. I've given him time to come to his senses. Maybe he needs me to come to mine. I refuse to let this love go, as if it was some shallow thing. I'm going to go get him. And the man is coming back with me, if I have to beg, scream, cry, or run naked through the city. There's no weakness in my faith.

All the way from the airport to his house is a practice in staying calm. It's not nerves or doubt that makes my stomach twist. It's excitement. That is how sure I am.

The Uber driver makes the final turn onto the property.

How strange. It seems like I have been gone for years, not weeks. Like I have arrived in a new world. My senses notice it all. Something is different. Maybe everything. What has made each thing change? The warmth of sunlight on the Sycamores was always there. The way the birds are flying in perfect harmony in the big sky? I've seen it countless times. But change has happened. It's the big picture, all consuming, magical feeling that settles in my heart.

We take the final curve in the road leading to the house, and a car I don't recognize approaches with someone in the backseat. As we come closer, it slows.

"Wait, driver!"

We slow to a crawl. And as the cars pass, time slows too. Our eyes meet and lock at the exact same moment. He says something to the driver, just as I say to mine.

"Stop!"

There's a frenzied excitement to get out of the car and into each other's arms. I throw the door open and slide out. Nobel's door won't budge, and he yells impatiently to the driver, who pops the lock. He's out. Kissing me, touching my hair. Saying everything in a look. His embrace is like slipping a key into the front door. We both have tears in our eyes.

He leans in, holds me close and whispers, "I don't want to be invisible anymore."

My lips graze his ear and I whisper back, "You won't be. I've come to wreck your plans and take you home."

We were born to walk this life together, the two of us. In perfect parallels and intersecting lines.

I kiss the man who fell to earth for me.

EPILOGUE
Nobel

One year later

I didn't know what love was. A clueless stranger in a strange land. But I got educated on what to cling to and what to let go. Now I think I could write the prologue of a book about how it shapes a man. It would be a bestseller. I sound like a fucking fool waxing poetic, and maybe I am. But this past year has schooled me in the art of the beginning.

Dove has schooled me. Just by example.

The woman knows how to love. I feel it when I'm with her and carry it when we are apart. I am sure of it, despite knowing some have come to regret the naïveté of being so certain. Love has fallen apart for lovers where no doubt existed. Smoke getting in their eyes. That's not us.

We look with clear vision, at both the magic and the mundane. Knowing our love is forever has made me trust the journey. The more I surrender, the further it takes me. I have left all thoughts of the world that was before.

There's nothing routine about our lives. Never thought

that would be a plus. Not when sameness was my previous default setting. Thought it was my comfort zone, right along with solitude. Shortsightedness was the problem. Living in the comfort zone has nothing on living fully in the moment.

I have grown to like the uniqueness of each city. Even crowds of fans can be fun, if controlled. And whenever it becomes too loud or crazy for my tastes, I find a way to quiet. I can be alone anytime I want. Nothing holds me back from doing my own thing. Thing is, I don't want to that often. To that end, taking a year-long sabbatical from the law has worked great. Next month I start back, and it will feel good to have my own thing to concentrate on again. Allegedly. I will see.

We have come full circle tonight. The return to McCandy's for the band's tip of the hat. The club that gave Montana their break was all too happy to agree to a one-night appearance from music's newest find. There has been no announcement or heads up to the public. That would have been a colossal mistake. Instead, we figured out seating for our friends and families, the VIP's of our lives, and advertised as if the patrons will be seeing a new group. The reputation of the club tells them whoever appears here is going to put on a good show. The usual crowds are anticipated.

When I peeked outside to see the patrons gathering, I noticed two old friends. The girls that were in line with me that first night are here again. How cool. Only their hair has changed. One sports a pink do and the other blonde. Hope they get inside. If not, I'm going to make sure it happens.

Two number one hits on the pop chart that segued into the country category has changed everything. The Archangel tour last November put Montana on the world's stage. It was a huge success for them. That was Michael Angelica's smartest move. It won't happen again. They are too big. But right before they broke out, he had them as his opening act. That alone is another angel feather in his cap.

Now there's talk of a national tour next year, but this time Montana will be the headliners. Their debut album is climbing the charts. I don't see anything stopping plans to perform from San Francisco to New York, and many cities in between.

Dove has become everyone's golden girl. But she is my woman. It's weird being photographed as a couple. Funny. The shoot for Entertainment Tonight's online magazine was a new experience. Getting praised for my looks, an embarrassment. It's happening pretty regularly now. Aargon, Scarlett, and Van will never let it die. They find it hysterically inaccurate. My birthday cake a few months ago said *Don't Get A Big Head, You Are Forty Fucking Five.* The words of my father when the article appeared, and I started getting compliments.

Inside Dove's dressing room, she dresses and I watch. Love to hang out while she prepares. She likes it too. Regularly, it turns into sex. They all know if the door is a lockin' don't come a knockin'. We are as annoying as eighteen-year-olds.

Knock knock.

"Thirty minutes to show," the backstage manager calls.

"That looks great, honey," I say, checking out the new outfit she just climbed into.

"Thanks. Does it make my ass look too big?"

"Turn around," I say, pretending I don't know the answer. "Your ass looks the perfect size. Not too small, not a watermelon."

She chuckles and blows me a kiss.

"Not that watermelon would be a bad thing. It's one of my favorites," I add.

Another knock.

"Yes?" she calls.

"It's me. Nobel in there?" Jimmy's voice needs no further introduction.

"I'm here. Come in."

The door swings open.

"Hey, can I steal your husband for a minute?"

We have gotten used to being called husband and wife by the band. Even though it is not legally a fact.

I follow him out the door and he heads for his dressing room.

"I have your birthday present. I'm a little late."

"I thought you did it on purpose. Just because you can be a dick."

"You are going to feel really shitty when you see what it is."

How this relationship morphed surprised me more than any other. I always felt an ease with Tony and Oscar. And even ZZ, whose bark is worse than his bite. Jimmy was something else. Because of his history with Dove, we both had our doubts. I initially thought we would *never* be friends.

But one thing changed, and her name is Polly. Arthur's receptionist. I'm not surprised at how thoroughly a woman can change a man. After all, it happened to me. But Jimmy, I think that one felt like it came out of the blue.

We reach the door, and he leads the way inside.

"So is this a gag gift or a real one?"

"A gag gift is a real one if you do it right. But no, this one is something you will like. I hope."

Leaning against the wall is a large canvas with its back to us. He picks it up and turns it to face me.

"Oh, man. God. That's…it's perfect, Jimmy. You did this?"

A smile lifts the corners of his mouth and he knows without a doubt he has scored a home run. Maudie's sweet face stares back at me. Somehow Jimmy captured her soul through the eyes. She is sitting above the River, under the trees, overlooking her kingdom. The wind is in the leaves and against her coat. She lifts her head loving the feel of the breeze.

"It's fucking beautiful, man. Thank you so much."

"Dove said you liked the one I did of her, so I figured I'd give this a try."

"You painted the one hanging in her grandparents' house?"

"Yeah."

I had no idea my favorite painting was Jimmy's creation. But it makes sense. He got the eyes right.

"It's beautiful, man. And this one is too."

My eyes get misty looking at Maudie's face again. Seeing her spirit. I come in for a quick hug. Not the first one we have shared in a year of knowing each other, but the most heartfelt.

"Don't cry, bro. You big baby."

My chuckle hides what I really feel in the moment. Here is my brother from another mother. Or another life where he called me a baby too.

The stage manager stops at the open door.

"Jimmy, I need to speak with you for a minute. Excuse us, Nobel."

"I'm outta here. Thanks, man. I love it."

"Good."

I grab the oil painting and head out.

"Here! Nobel sit here!" my father calls above the din of the club. He waves me over to the group of tables where my family sits. There wasn't any big enough for the Lyon's and their guests. So, they got creative and pushed four together.

I take the three steps off the stage and snake through the happy patrons, most in the dark as to who will be performing.

There was no billboard outside or online news. That alone should spark their imaginations.

Just as I'm about to reach my family, a hand grabs my wrist. It's pink hair. The friend sits with an arm around her shoulders. Ah. Girlfriends.

"We meet again," I say, smiling my recognition.

"You remember us then?"

"Yeah, I do. That was a good night. How you girls doing?"

Pinky lifts her left hand and shows off a ring.

"We're engaged. Hey. Who are we going to see?"

A grin proceeds the answer. "I'm not sure. And congratulations!"

"Bullshit," she whispers. "We've seen you on TMZ with," she looks around before continuing. "With you know who."

"I can neither confirm nor deny," I say chuckling.

Their eyes widen and I see the excitement rise. Pinky squeezes her girlfriend's hand. I lean down and give a final message.

"Keep it to yourselves. We don't want a stampede outside."

"We noticed the extra security! I'm so excited!" Blondie says, ignoring my directive.

I tilt my head giving a firmer order. "Come on. Behave yourselves for another five minutes."

"Okay, okay! We hear you."

"Good. Have fun, girls," I say, walking away. One of them squeals their excitement. I shake my head.

"Hey! This is going to be fun. Hi," I say, taking my place with the family.

"What you want to drink?" Aargon says. "Whiskey?"

I'm almost rendered silent as I surreptitiously try to figure out who he has an arm around. A woman. Jesus.

"Yeah, that's good. Introduce me to your dates," I say, bringing Van into the mix.

"This is Addie. Addie this is Nobel," Aargon says with an expression I haven't seen in years.

Then Van pops in with his latest interest. "And this is Diedre."

"Hi, Diedre, Addie. Glad to meet you both," I practically have to shout.

The noise in the room is growing. Anticipation. It's hard to hear each other at this point. Our conversation will consist of expressions and body language at this point.

Out of nowhere my father grabs my face and plants a big one on my cheek.

All I can do is laugh.

The lights dim and the room illuminates with energy. They are going crazy before they know who is coming to the stage.

"Ladies and gentlemen, you are about to be verrrrry excited!" The familiar baritone voice announces his prize. "You will talk about this night for years to come. McCandy's welcomes back to the stage, the one and only, Montana!!!!"

Oh shit! The place goes wild. Screams and whistles, as the curtains pull back revealing the band. Dove opens her arms to the room and the guys begin to play their first number one song, "Mined". It comes to me that they are the same as they were that first night. The same talent, sexual appeal, just as dedicated and one-minded in their art. The public just needed to find them.

Now, as they sing the chorus, the audience joins in. Singing along, knowing every word of the clever combination of notes that have captured people's attention. I love it and so do the band members. Dove is playing the stage, picking a person to focus on for a minute. She goes from one side to the other, engaging her fans.

The guys do their thing, varying little from what I watched a year ago. Tony still checks out the fresh meat, and

Oscar stays in his mind, feeling the music. ZZ beats the rhythm with the same one-minded aim. Getting lost in the drums. Jimmy, he may be the only one who is in a different headspace. I catch him looking at his girl and not being able to control his smile.

So much has happened in a year.

As the song ends and the applause dies, Dove speaks.

"Hello, McCandy's!! We are so happy to perform for you tonight! We want to thank you for your steady affection. Here's a song you might remember us singing. It was our most requested, a year ago."

"Wild Thing's" opening chords play, and again the crowd explodes with energy.

I catch the eye of my mother, who sends me a wink and a nod. Then she locks eyes with my father and smiles. Her own wild thing.

Sunlight streaks across the room and illuminates her face. Being in my house again feels better than good. Maybe because it's rare that we are here. In the last year it's only been a handful of times. That has made the coming home, if even for a few days, kind of magical. I remember how I felt the first time I saw the property. It's like that again. I'll never sell this place. It has become touchstone, not just for me, but for both of us. Thank God.

"I wish we had another few days here," Dove says, wiping the sleep out of her eyes. "We could go fishing."

"Are you really thinking about trout when I'm laying here naked?"

She rolls against me and crosses her arms on my chest.

"No baby. It's just that your squirming cock reminded me of a fish jumping."

That fucking look that she gets whenever she talks about

my dick. Like it is her favorite toy. It's an aphrodisiac. I push the conversation aside and get to more interesting things. Like her ass and pussy, the beautiful breasts and the softness of her skin. And how she smells like a summer morning.

"Come here," I say, touching my lips.

She abandons talk of anything outside this room, this bed, and takes the kiss. Nothing in this world compares to how it feels to make love to Dove. To have her make love to me. She paints with all the colors. Words are an injustice.

I throw the bedding back and start a tour of her body. Lovely thing that it is. My hands wander over the wonderland. Fuck. Those nipples. They are in my mouth before I finish the thought. Babe. There is nothing like making love slowly. Like walking without a destination. Just for the journey's pure pleasure.

Getting between my legs, she climbs my body with kisses. When she presses her mouth to my nipples I wish I could absorb her in my skin.

It is strange to want the thing you already have. But that's the gold. We *want* each other. My pulse picks up its beat as she meets my stare. The feel of that sweet pussy grabs ahold of my senses.

"You fucking goddess," I say between clenched teeth.

One second later, she turns and climbs on top of me. Backwards. Oh Lord. The perfect ass right in front of me. I part her cheeks and see the wet, soft pussy lips, I see it all. My mouth takes its share of the bounty, licking and sucking. While she worships my dick. That's what it feels like. Like she has made a god of it and vowed allegiance.

With my hands on her bouncing breasts, I continue to feast. Her pussy tastes so good. I lick from top to bottom. Taking my dick, she rubs it against her nipples, and it makes me hard as fuck. Then she sits back on my face and wiggles a request.

I'm happy to oblige. I eat that sweet thing and taste the slick juices that result. Rolling her over, I make an instant decision. Want to see that gorgeous face while we fuck. Kiss her. Hear the sounds that escape parted lips. And I am not disappointed.

We do it on our sides, on top, on her stomach, me on my knees, her on my lap. I hold her head back and we kiss while my dick is inside her. My orgasm delayed as long as possible. She came twice. Just another day in Paradise.

"Let's never let this go," she says softly.

Then we laugh because it's a ridiculous thought. My eyes take their due, looking at my heaven.

"Want to have coffee out on the porch? It looks like a beautiful day."

"Yes. Let's."

This right here is what floats my boat. A big cup of strong black coffee and a view. Maudie and I used to sit out here staring at the majestic scene. Today it looks especially stunning.

"Love this," Dove says, lifting her feet onto the railing.

"Love you," I answer.

We sit in silence, taking in the details. The sun highlighting the mountains, the colors of the flowering plants. There are so many shades of green. The tree leaves, the shrubs, the variegated vegetation. Turning my head, I look out over the far vista, where river meets shore.

A feeling rushes through me. Like a wind. I have felt this before but had forgotten. It was when Dove sang to me that first time. Does it mean something important is happening? Or is it only reaction to extreme beauty?

"Whose hat is that?" Dove's question breaks my focus.

She points to the basket of hats I keep on the porch for visitors who want some shade.

"Which one?"

"The purple one with the pink band. Who does that belong to?"

"It was Kristen's. I can't get rid of it, so I threw it in the pile. We'd sit out here and solve the world's problems."

The oddest look comes over her face. She wants to tell me something, I can see it in her eyes.

"I've seen her. Several times."

"What?"

"My visions. I thought I was seeing you with another woman. She was touching your shoulder or arm. But it was always from the back. I never saw her face. Once she was touching a toddler. Oh my God."

Chills run up my spine. And a feeling of happiness wraps itself around me.

"Wow. I'm stunned a little. Did she look happy?"

"She was happy. Being with you made her really happy. I could see that without hesitation."

"Who was the kid?" I say, coming to my own conclusion.

She doesn't answer, but just looks in my eyes and smiles.

"Ours?" I ask.

"Who knows?"

The sense of wind blowing through me, and clearing away every unnecessary thought, returns.

Listen, it says.

And I do. Now is the time. As Dove waits and watches for my reaction, I respond with the only thing that has been on my mind for months.

"Will you marry me?"

The words float on the wind and settle in her eyes. She knew. Of course, she knew.

ALSO BY LESLIE PIKE

The Paradise Series
The Trouble With Eden
Wild In Paradise
The Road To Paradise

Love In Italy
The Adventure
The Art Of Love *

Swift Series
The Curve
The Closer
The Cannon
The Swift Collection

Santini Series
Destiny Laughs
Destiny Plays
Destiny Shines
Destiny Dawns

Lyon Family Series
The Beach In Winter
The River In Spring *

Standalones (for now)

7 Miles High *

Royal Pain * (Cocky Hero Club)

Until Now (Happily Ever After World and Swift Family Crossover)

* Available in audio

ABOUT THE AUTHOR

USA TODAY bestselling author, Leslie Pike, has loved expressing herself through the written word since she was a child. The first romance "book" she wrote was at ten years old. The scene, a California Beach. The hero, a blonde surfer. The ending, happily forever after.

Leslie's passion for film and screenwriting eventually led her to Texas for eight years, writing for a prime time CBS series. She's traveled the world as part of film crews, from Africa to Israel, New York to San Francisco. Now she finds her favorite creative adventures taking place in her home, in Southern California, writing Contemporary Romance.

Connect With Leslie:
www.lesliepike.com

Made in the USA
Monee, IL
31 May 2021